HESTER'S DREAM

WITH SOME OF THE NOTABLE RESIDENTS OF HINTON COURT

*To Dearest Caroline
with love from
Nicky ♡.*

Cover and illustration on page 103 by Nicola Masiello

For Anne – the Instigator.

PREFACE

Following the death of my wife in 2010, I became the "Lifetime Resident" of a converted water tower in the grounds of what was once film mogul J Arthur Rank's Sutton Manor – now a nursing home, part of the Amesbury Abbey Group. Within the 60 acre grounds the late Mary Cornelius Reid, MBE had accommodation built for Independent Living Residents, some of whom form the basis for the characters depicted here. However it must be emphasised that *Hester's Dream* is a mixture of fact and fiction.

TdVC, 2023

CHAPTER 1

Nineteen eighty-seven. The year of the Great Storm.

The eyelids of an elderly male hospital patient fluttered and opened to a view of the ceiling. A nurse's head appeared.

"Hello Mr Garfield – you're in the recovery room after your operation we'll soon have you back in your room. Would you like something to drink?"

In the corridor of a private hospital, 'The Tower', Gerald Garfield, on a trolley, is pushed to his room.

Colin Clift, a Consultant Oncologist in his forties, having finished looking at his notes and shuffled them into their folder, has risen with an air of finality.

Gerald, now settled in his room, turned off the television as Colin Clift, with the folder, shut the door and moved to sit by his bed.

"The operation went well. We removed the tumour and cleaned up where we could but I'm sorry to have to tell you that the cancer has spread to such an extent – liver, kidneys, colon – that any further operation would be fatal. It's terminal."

Having taken this in, Gerald asked: "How long have I got?" The reply was: "Could be weeks, could be months. We can fix you up with painkillers, and when the time comes, book you into a hospice for final palliative care. Meanwhile, we'll get you home in a week."

Hester Rachel Foster, a nurse in her late twenties, best described as handsome and attractive, with a face that indicated a strong character, was gestured to sit opposite 'The Tower's' Matron, Jane Wright, at her desk.

"I've chosen you to look after a patient who has just been told by Mr Clift that he has terminal cancer and who will be here for a week, before he goes home."

She looked down at her notes.

"Gerald Garfield is eighty-two, a widower, with next of kin listed as his elder sister, Rose, who is wheelchair-bound. His two sons, Paul and Philip, are married with families. One in Canada, one in Australia. He has told Mr Clift that he only wants them informed after his death."

Matron looked up.

"When he first met Mr Clift, he made it clear he could afford whatever was necessary for his private treatment. After that meeting Mr Clift researched him and found out he is the multi-millionaire who founded

Garfield Enterprises: early pioneers of modern computers. Mr Clift said that he took the news as well as could be expected, but obviously needs sympathetic handling. Alright?"

Hester nodded with a "yes".

Having introduced herself to Gerald, Hester told him she was on daytime call for anything she could do for him before he went home.

Gerald thanked her and then said: "The thing is I've got a home but no one to look after me. I thought I might not return and paid off my housekeeper. To be honest, we were never suited and I'm not sure she'd want to return, even if I asked her. Has The Tower had similar cases? Do they have contacts with any firms who deal with care for terminal cases who don't want to go into hospices?"

Hester said she would find out.

Having told matron the situation, Hester said: "I like him and I feel we'd get on well. I'd like to say 'I'll look after you.' My question is, presuming he agrees, and it will be for a short time, would the hospital take me back?"

The immediate reply was: "Certainly, you're one of our best nurses."

Hester told Gerald there was a firm that provided the necessary qualified home carers but she had cleared it with Matron that she could look after him, if he'd like her to. He looked surprised but said he would be delighted if she did.

The partnership was a success. Gerald's large flat was at the Knightsbridge end of Sloane Street,

London SW1. Hester moved into what had been the housekeeper's quarters: bedroom, bathroom, her own small kitchen and a sitting room with television. Gerald had an account at nearby Harrods and she enjoyed shopping there and cooking for him.

He had insisted that he pay her double the hospital wage and the arrangement was that on alternate weekends, a qualified carer from the firm known to the hospital, would cover for Hester, allowing her to lead her own life: to return to the flat she shared with another nurse, visit her parents, or take a break elsewhere.

He gradually deteriorated, as expected, but was not a difficult patient. He appreciated her company and finding out about her. How she came from a humble but loving family; father a lorry driver, mother a cleaner, and how one brother was a merchant seaman and the other a gardener with Battersea Council. How she started, aged sixteen, as a skivvy in the hospital kitchens and at eighteen became a trainee nurse.

After four months, sounding and looking visibly weaker, Gerald called Hester and asked her to sit down.

"You've been wonderful looking after me but I think the time has come for me to go."

Hester looked enquiringly at him.

"To die. Don't worry, I'm not going to ask you to

give me a pill. I know of such a thing actually happening. My wife Anne's Scottish grandmother was in her nineties when she said to Anne's mother 'It's time I was gathered,' quickly followed by 'Och, it's 'The Likely Lads' tonight – I'll see them furst.' Then, true to her words, she died that night. I don't want to go to a hospice. Will you be able to cope?"

Hester bowed her head and nodded.

"What will you do when I'm gone?"

"I'll miss you."

"Yes, but will you go back to the hospital?"

"Yes."

"Will you want to get married and have children?"

"In due course."

"I sense you have ambition." He waited for a reply. "Come on – what for? I had dreams. You must have dreams."

She countered with: "I'll tell you mine if you tell me how yours worked out."

He gave a tired smile.

"Are you sitting comfortably? Then I'll begin."

"I was the first boy from my prep school to get a scholarship to Chichester College but I soon realised that I didn't fit and became something of a rebel. The headmaster spoke to my father and admitted that there were failures on the school's part and that I was clever. He suggested I go somewhere more suitable, a smaller school in Devon: Marwood, where the headmaster, Commander Thornhill, who had been a submariner in WWI, welcomed 'difficult but interesting' boys. His philosophy was that every boy could and should succeed in something.

Soon after arrival, I read under 'Rules' on the noticeboard, a small piece of paper with his initials, which solely stated 'a breach of common sense is a breach of school rules'.

After I left Chichester, a friend wrote mentioning that on Founder's Day the prizes had been presented by an Old Boy, now a bishop, who had ended his address by turning to those on the dais: 'To the staff I say: cherish your rebels.'

"At Marwood, with the help of an excellent maths teacher, I got a scholarship to Trinity College, Cambridge. The end result was a first class degree – when a first meant something.

"My parents suggested I become an accountant, pointing out that with that qualification a whole list of jobs would be open to me. But I had dreams and I didn't want to waste time qualifying. I got a job working in computing, then in its infancy. Hardly more than glorified calculators to start with. By the age of twenty-eight I had my own firm and was a millionaire. During the war I was at Bletchley Park. Breaking codes was difficult but rewarding work. The Germans believed that their "Enigma" was unbreakable. The Polish gave us the lead, and I was lucky enough to be a member of Alan Turing's team, which achieved the ultimate solution.

He looked at Hester.

"Now, what is your dream?"

She took a deep breath, exhaled, and said: "Okay.

I'd like to set up a high-quality nursing home, but with enough grounds to build, or convert existing buildings, into apartments for still active old people to retire to – with an independent life style but with back-up facilities."

Gerald nodded. "Well – certainly ambitious."

Hester shrugged. "Just a dream."

~

Gerald died the following week. Hester attended his funeral and soon returned to a warm welcome at the hospital. A month later, she received a letter asking her to confirm that she could attend a solicitor's office at a time of her choosing – coincidentally on the date of her birthday. Having consulted with Matron, she arrived to be greeted by the senior partner, a large bouquet of flowers and an envelope. James Murdoch, beckoned her to open it.

The enclosed card simply said: "Happy birthday. Fulfil your dream." And had a cheque for two million pounds attached.

Mr Murdoch smiled as she looked up at him in amazement. "Mr Garfield told me about you and gave me his instructions. His sons and their families have been well provided for. They know nothing of this arrangement and if they did I'm sure that they wouldn't make a fuss. He also asked my firm to act for you in any way we can and put aside a fund for that purpose – to fulfil your dream."

CHAPTER 2

Hester explained to Matron what had happened and how she intended to find a large house in the country, preferably at a low price, something which needed work, but suitable for conversion into a nursing home with potential for housing development in the grounds.

The matron wished her well and said she'd love to help in any way especially with advice setting up the nursing side.

Having passed her driving test aged nineteen, Hester bought a small car to enable her to view country properties.

One pair of eyes at the hospital soon noticed her absence. Tall, thirty-year-old doctor Sam Harvey had arrived at The Tower during Hester's time with Gerald Garfield. On her return he had soon 'clocked'

her and decided after a month to introduce himself. To his dismay, he was told she had left.

Having been given her address by Matron, he wrote and asked her out. He, in turn, had not gone unnoticed by Hester and she was pleased to accept. Over a candlelit dinner they realised that they were meant for each other and within six months, in the natural course of events, they got married.

As Hester Rachel Harvey (HRH), she acquired dilapidated Hinton Court, with twenty acres, near Salisbury. Built in the 19th century with lodge, barn, stables, a staff cottage and in the grounds, an artist's studio built in 1903.

The previous owner was an antiques dealer who had specialised in garden statuary and had been extradited to the USA where he was given a prison sentence for fraud. The property had been empty for over two years; stripped of all furniture and statuary to pay off debts.

With seven bedrooms on the first floor, four attic rooms, a large cellar that could be a storeroom, possible conversions of the barn, lodge, stables and studio, and with potential development within the grounds and ample parking space, it met her require-ments. Over time the price had been reduced and the estate agent reduced it further when it became apparent there were no complications – no depen-dence on a house sale or loans.

When Hester approached the local council with her ideas, they sensed a project that would help the local economy and boost employment. An architect was suggested who was aware of building requirements for a nursing home – ramps for wheelchairs, lifts, and so on.

On meeting Giles Hill at Hinton Court there was an immediate empathy. He showed her drawings and photographs of his work and she explained she would like to have up to twelve units in the main house (nursing home) all with their own bathrooms, varying from bedsits to suites with a sitting room and bedroom. The nursing home scheme was to incorporate the stable block and replace the large greenhouse, both attached to the house. She would agree if he thought it necessary to adjust the existing ground floor layout, as long as there was a large dining room with adjacent kitchen and an impressive sitting room with nearby cloakrooms. She realised the need for staff and treatment rooms.

When they left the house to tour the grounds, she explained she and her husband would live in the lodge at the entrance to the drive. And off the drive she would like a purpose-built Georgian stable style courtyard building of eight individual two-bedroom apartments, with varying layouts and small gardens. She asked for his suggestions for how the barn could be converted into apartments and he gave a big smile when he saw the studio.

She hoped for fifteen residential apartments and an admin building for both the nursing home and the residential apartments, to incorporate a small bedroom for the duty warden. Hester felt it essential to have a warden on site 24/7. The area to be chosen by Giles. Also a pavilion, equivalent to a village hall, for residents' meetings and entertaining, with library, art classes, bridge club, book club, yoga, if possible, placed near a croquet lawn.

She left him to go round the buildings and grounds on his own, measuring up and sketching ideas, telling him that he would find her in the existing main sitting room. When he eventually knocked on the door, he found her at a table surrounded by papers, making lists of staff requirements. He promised to deliver rough drawings with ideas and a provisional estimate within a week.

As they were walking to his car , he stopped and said: "All this is going to cost a massive amount. Forgive me, but aren't you being over ambitious?" She smiled. "Maybe, but I have a rich backer," – she looked skyward – "no longer with us." And without naming figures she told Giles that Gerald Garfield was enabling her to fulfil her dream.

Hester asked her brother Jack to move, in due course, into the cottage with his wife, Bridget, and their two young children. He to be head gardener/groundsman with an increased salary from that paid by Battersea Council. Bridget, who had been a secretary, was happy to work in the office.

Hester and Sam had some minor alterations made to the Lodge, by a builder recommended by Giles, and then moved from London, Sam having become a

GP and joined the local surgery that would serve as Hinton Court's surgery.

After discussions and adjustments, plans were submitted and approved in three months. Work began immediately and was completed internally and externally in eight months, just over budget, with help from Gerald Garfield's solicitor's fund. The barn was now six apartments on two floors with a lift.

While searching for a suitable property, Hester had visited various nursing homes, on the premise of looking on behalf of her recently widowed grand-mother. She collected brochures and, at one with apartments in the grounds, a sample copy of a resi-dential agreement. She studied "Some Frequently Asked Questions".

What does the quarterly service charge include?

The quarterly charge is made to cover the cost of services and facilities including a twice-weekly domestic help and a warden service 24/7.

What assistance is provided by the warden?

The warden acts as a friend and good neighbour and will assist in an emergency to offer advice and ensure that relatives, GPs or the emergency services are notified, as appropriate, if required.

What is included in the twice-weekly domestic help element of the charge?

You can determine what you require; cleaning, laundry, vacuuming, etc. Your rubbish will also be collected as part of this service.

May I bring my pet with me?

Residents may keep a pet subject to two conditions. Firstly, prior permission should be obtained in writing. Secondly, the pet should not cause a nuisance to neighbours, other residents, or the owner's business.

May I plant anything in the garden?

Yes, with approval from the owner and in consultation with our head groundsman, residents can contribute to the planting of gardens adjacent to their properties. Trees and shrubs, however, cannot be planted or altered without wider consultation in the interest of other residents.

Do I have access to the nursing home in case of illness?

Short spells of illness can be catered for within the nursing home and, wherever possible, we will give priority to residents should these services be required.

Hester sent all the paperwork and brochures to James Murdoch, asking that his firm draw up a similar agreement for her. When she went to see him, he pointed out various additional legal requirements and then suggested a major amendment.

At the 'set up' she had visited with properties in the grounds, they had been bought with the understanding that when the resident left to go into the nursing home, or died, any potential new buyer/occupier could be vetoed by the nursing home's owner or owners. This could lead to disputes. He suggested what he called a 'Lifetime Residency.' That, basically, a deposit was put down on the property by the resident which, on leaving, would be returned. No deficit or increase, however long they had been in residence. Importantly, the property would remain in Hester's hands to accept a new resident of her choice and the leaving resident, or their executors, need have no concern about estate agents and selling the property. She would be responsible for the building's insurance and maintenance and the garden's upkeep: costs covered in the quarterly service charge.

Hester was fortunate that in the 1990s, nursing homes with set-ups such as hers were rare and Giles had alerted a journalist friend, who wrote a comprehensive article, complete with photographs, about Hinton Court. This was printed in the *Salisbury Journal* and engendered interest in the national press and magazines, such as *The Oldie* and *House and Home*.

Enquiries and visits by potential inmates, for both the nursing home and the residential apartments, were soon mounting up and concluding successfully.

In the nursing home, families of an elderly relative were shown round by Jane Wright, the ex-'Tower' Matron. She had visited at an early stage of development to see how things were progressing and, having consulted with her husband, a teacher, who was happy to move to the Salisbury area, she asked if she could be involved. Hester was delighted and immediately employed her as Matron and to recruit staff.

For the post of Head Warden (there would be three wardens), Jane recommended an experienced colleague, Emma Robinson, who, having worked extensively as a carer for the NHS, was now the organiser of a department which specialised in complex cases, such as autism and mental health issues. A strong but sympathetic character who was looking for something different.

Soon after building work had started, Emma was approached and she visited Hinton Court. After a tour and meeting with Hester, she was offered employment as Head Warden, to start in four months' time. Having had a discussion with her husband, a jobbing builder, she said that they were happy to move, and asked if he could be involved in the maintenance side – which he duly was.

CHAPTER 3

The first potential resident to arrive for an inspection was Fabia Denby, who stepped out of her eye-catching old drop-head Alvis with what she would have called "positivity."

When Hester asked her, during the tour, what she did in the war, she replied: "I was at Bletchley Park." Hester stopped and asked : "I wonder if you knew Gerald Garfield?" The answer was: "Oh yes – delightful man. But I was an administrator, not a codebreaker. People only think of Bletchley Park with a select group of codebreakers led by Alan Turing, yet everyone of the thousands involved had an important role, however small, and eighty percent were women. My main job was to make sure those who worked odd and long hours were well looked after. Bletchley Park continued to function after the war, but with consider-ably fewer staff. I was one of those organising the reduction."

When Fabia Denby had gone, having booked

"Larkspur" in the stable block (all eight apartments were named after Derby winners, Larkspur from 1962) Hester found out that she was the unmarried daughter of a high court judge.

In 1947 she had become the main assistant of the flamboyant archaeologist, Sir Aubrey Greville Cook, famous for his excavation of the Iron Age hill fort at Stoke Minster in Dorset. AGC, as he was known to his work force, genuinely believed that our past was relevant and should be available to everyone. He encouraged the public to visit his digs. But there were those in his profession who called him "Flash Harry" and a self-promoter.

In his report AGC wrote "Vespasian, the future Emperor, came with the Second Legion to England in AD 43. It is chronicled that he defeated the Durotriges tribe, and took their capital, Stoke Minster. A skull, which had received nine cuts suggests the fury of a massacre. The bodies must have been buried by fellow Britons, since they were accompanied by food bowls and mugs. Many of them still wore such ornaments as armlets and finger- and toe-rings, and a warrior had been allowed to take his battle-axe and knife."

This was archaeology at its most vivid, and the crowds came in their hundreds. The local pressmen presented AGC with a silver cigarette box, in gratitude for him having enabled them to give their readers "archaeology without tears."

Fabia's job description would have been to assist and organise AGC's daily schedules. Over the years she also found herself, at various times, being a field assistant, dealing with transport and lodgings for the unit, and helping with complicated pay days. In the post-war years students had replaced labourers on excavations and were apt to come and go irregularly.

The 'personal' aspect was also in evidence. AGC was known as an active man with "the ladies." There were girl students on his digs who came to Fabia in tears. She had the courage to face AGC and warn him of his actions. When he took no notice, she told him if he did not stop she would report him to the police. The threat worked, helped by the arrival in a visiting group of the beautiful, blonde, promiscuous actress Julia Jones, who became his second wife; he her third husband. She discovered that she did not enjoy "being thrust into archaeology" and there were tempestuous rows.

During a dig in France she disappeared. Eventually she telephoned Fabia – with whom she had a good relationship – "I suppose you'd better come and fetch me." When told AGC thought, correctly, she had been with a lover and asked if he could borrow Fabian's new Alvis to retrieve her. The reply was "Only if you borrow me too, as driver." On the way he remarked "You see some chocolates and you have to have them, even if you know you will be sick afterwards."

After the divorce that soon followed, Julia and Fabia remained friends. So when, four years later, Julia was sent on remand to Holloway, the women's prison, having been implicated in a drugs war during which two thugs had been shot dead, it was Fabia who immediately reacted. She rang a welfare worker friend who advised she contact the prison chaplain for help. Having written a letter to Julia, enclosing another letter which she could send to Fabia's solicitor, if she thought it necessary, Fabia arrived at the prison built in 1852. Designed like a castle, it was still a grim place. (Closed in 2016). Fabia banged on the studded door until they let her in. After a bit of a battle, her insistence that she see the chaplain was granted, and he agreed to get the letter to Julia.

Throughout the protracted legal process, the trial and the six month sentence, Fabia was a support, not just to Julia, but to Mark, her young son by her first husband, who had been killed at Dunkirk during the May 1940 evacuation.

Soon after Fabia had settled in at Hinton Court, Mark, now a grandfather, came down with his family, the first of many visits, when his two young grandchildren always clamoured for a repeat of the first time Fabia took them out "for a spin" in the hood down Alvis.

Another early arrival for an inspection was a tall gentleman in his early eighties with a moustache and a monocle, whose bearing suggested a military man. Indeed, Hester was to have confirmation of this at his eventual memorial service in St Paul's, Covent Garden, the actor's church in London, that, as an officer, he had been one of the first to lead the D-Day Normandy landings, and had been awarded a Military Cross.

He had not rung to make an appointment and arrived on his own. He gave his name as Willoughby Green, an actor – "You may have seen me in supporting roles on television". Hester remembered that he had been a semi-regular in the popular series *Boatbuilders,* portraying an up-market merchant banker, Sir John Ponsonby, who had amusing scenes with jumped-up 'Medallion Man', Ken Moss, who owned the local chandlery.

At present, Mr Green was living in Laverstock on the outskirts of Salisbury. His wife had died two months previously, and his family, two sons and a daughter, had all left the nest some time ago.

When shown The Studio he immediately said that it would suit him nicely – he was an artist and the conversion, which had divided the large, north-facing window with an inserted first floor, was perfect. He would put his house on the market straight away and hope that no one else would want the place and be able to take it before him.

When Willo (as he was known to his friends) brought his family for an inspection, they were impressed, though when one son asked if he had looked at any other properties – those all on one level with two bedrooms and two bathrooms – he admitted he had not. But his daughter said the stairs to the bedroom would be good exercise for him, and with the additional downstairs loo and a pull-out sofa he could accept visitors.

The sale of Willo's house progressed quickly and after three months he was installed in The Studio at Hinton Court.

Within a year, the nursing home's twelve units were taken and a waiting list had been started. Similarly, the fifteen apartments in the grounds were occupied, also with a waiting list.

At the community's daily lunches, unlike some residents who were considered bores when recounting their lives, Willo was a popular raconteur – laughter flowing from whatever table he was allocated. For those who hadn't heard them, he was asked to repeat his *Waterloo* stories.

Willo and his friend Jeremy Neville (an Old Etonian), were cast as officers in the Ukrainian director Sergei Bondarchuk's 1970 film, with Rod Steiger as Napoleon and Christopher Plummer as Wellington. In the considerable intervals between being required, Willo and Jeremy (who would only ever be allocated posh parts) were to be seen sitting together in their uniforms, quietly knitting.

An appreciation of Jeremy Neville by a former General Secretary of Equity, the actor's union, read: "If anyone had told Jeremy that he was a trade union activist a look of utter incredulity would have descended upon that handsome face. Nevertheless, he served decades on the Equity Council and, encouraged by others to stand, found himself elected as President of the union for a two year term."

Willo, in addition to his acting role, was also hired as military adviser on *Waterloo*. When he pointed out to the director that on the battlefield the officers would not be wearing the same uniforms they had worn at the previous night's Duchess of Richmond's ball, Sergei Bondarchuk said with a smile: "You know it's wrong, and now I know it's wrong, but who else will know it's wrong?"

With no Wikipedia or Google at that time, Hester did not fully comprehend Willo's accomplishments until they were revealed at his memorial service. He was a professional illustrator of school history books and an expert on heraldry and medieval history. The cover for the memorial service showed Willo's drawing of the blind King of Bohemia at the 1346 battle of Crecy and he was the winner of an Emmy for his television documentary on that subject.

CHAPTER 4

For many of Hester's residents, the Second World War had provided the most exciting time in their lives.

At the funeral service, in the packed local church, of the gentle, kind, and wise Helena Tregunna, widow of a vicar, she was revealed to have been, during the war, with the Special Operations Executive (SOE), part of Churchill's 'secret army' designed to conduct subversion and espionage in occupied Europe – to "set Europe alight". She became an agent and had been flown into France, having been trained in combat and commando tactics, to parachute behind enemy lines, lead the Resistance fighters and blow up communications.

Helena had left school at seventeen and then been sent by her upper-class parents to a finishing school in Paris, where she became a fluent French speaker, before returning to London for debutante parties, combined with a secretarial course.

As an 'English Rose' beauty of nineteen, in 1941 she joined the counter intelligence and double-agent section of MI5. A family friend in the War Office had recommended that she be interviewed. She had been impressive and was immediately asked to sign the Official Secrets Act, going on to work in the section which gathered, filtered, and analysed Ultra decrypts, Abwehr messages and other intelligence, to be used in the running of double agents and the double-cross system.

She was given the job of sorting through 'Yellow Perils'; yellow carbon copies of interrogations from Camp 20, the wartime internment centre in Richmond, near London, where all enemy spies were grilled. She would read the accounts given by those captured and try to spot anything that required the attention of her senior (male) colleagues. It was Helena who identified 'glowing inconsistencies' in the confession of a French prisoner, who was then found to be a triple agent.

Her intelligence, discernment and acumen was noted and she was told to report to an address in Baker Street. After an extensive round of interviews and having her French tested, she was asked to join the SOE.

In 1943 she fell in love with a fellow agent and, after a short engagement, they were married. He was soon sent on a mission from which he did not return. After the war, German documents showed that following capture and interrogation, he had revealed nothing of consequence and had been shot.

Helena found comfort in her Christian faith and in particular with a vicar whose wife and family had been killed by a V1 flying bomb, known as a 'Doodle-bug'. He became a rock for her and she for him.

It was her son, also a priest, who conducted her funeral and told her story, on a clear, cold morning, to a mostly astonished congregation.

A close friend of Helena's who also had an exciting war was the no-nonsense and handsome Sybil Fane-Lloyd. She disclosed something of her background when at lunch a male fellow resident had boasted how, after the war, his mother had come out to Malta and been taken for a day out on a Royal Navy Motor Torpedo Boat (MTB). This sparked: "I was taken out in a submarine". Sybil was persuaded to explain that during the war, when a Wren in Malta, she had been responsible for sending and receiving coded signals to and from submarines when they surfaced at night in the Mediterranean.

Whilst at Cheltenham Ladies' College, aged 17, she was one of the two girls selected by the head-mistress for interviewing by a "man from the Ministry". After a second interview she was sent to Farley Court, near Henley, to learn about codes and ciphers and to master high speed Morse transmissions of at least twenty words per minute. There was a high dropout rate for wireless operators but she passed and, after learning to transmit and receive signals under wartime conditions at a specialised school in Scotland, she wrote with excitement to her family that she was being posted abroad. She did not mention that it was to Malta.

No doubt the submariners were grateful for her efficiency and, when they met her, they would have been struck by the attractiveness of this young Wren. Indeed she married one of them. He survived the war and reached the rank of Captain. She enjoyed being a naval attaché's wife, in appointments as diverse as Oman and Oslo.

Now a widow and adored grandmother, she was a member of many of Hinton Court's activities, and enjoyed swapping naval memories with Commander Harrow, who had served with her husband.

CHAPTER 5

Commander George Henry Harrow DSC was an unassuming war hero, whose actions had helped change the course of the Battle of the Atlantic, and therefore, World War II. As a midshipman he had been part of the team that captured the enigma machine and was mentioned in *The Times* obituary of David Balme:

Leader of the operation which captured the Enigma cipher machine and helped win the Second World War.
On 9th May 1941 Sub-Lieutenant David Balme shouted the order to lower the ship's sea-boat into the swelling mid-Atlantic. Three hundred yards across the waves there wallowed his destination, a stricken German U-boat, stern down.
Balme and his men were from the British destroyer Bulldog, *the leading ship in the 3rd Escort Group accompanying convoy OB318. Her fellow escorting*

vessel, the corvette HMS Aubretia, had forced the U-boat to surface with depth charges, and Bulldog's gunfire had damaged her. She had been abandoned by her crew. The armed boarding party which rowed across had orders to strip her of anything useful. Balme formed his men into a chain to pass out books and documents when a midshipman [George Harrow] called out: "This looks like an interesting bit of equipment, sir." It resembled a typewriter but lit up strangely when the midshipman pressed the keys. It was a German naval 'Enigma' cipher machine. The party found daily settings and procedures for its use. Written in soluble ink, they risked being lost if dropped in the sea, but Balme recalled: "Nothing got wet."

The machine and documents helped turn looming defeat in the Battle of the Atlantic to victory. For much of the war's first two years, when Britain stood alone, U-boat attacks sank too many ships bringing vital supplies. "The only thing that really frightened me during the war was the U-boat peril," Winston Churchill recorded.

The U-110 story emerged only in the 1970s. There was anger in Britain when, in 2000, the American director Jonathan Mostow made a film starring Harvey Keitel and Jon Bon Jovi which renumbered the U-boat "571" and pretended that US sailors had made the find. Balme reflected that before Hollywood made the film, no one had heard of the episode.

A popular character, George took the role of Chairman at the residents' meetings in The Pavilion.

This he did especially well, with wit and humour, when diverse opinions were strongly expressed during discussions about the Christmas collection for gratuities to the staff.

~

Hinton Court unwittingly fostered quite a few romantic liaisons for those in their sunset years. Though now an elderly widower, George was still an attractive man and although much admired by many of the ladies, he was particularly attracted to Charlotte Houston.

Soon after she arrived, George heard that her maiden name was Keir and that she was the daughter of a renowned naval captain, Edward Keir, who had engaged the German battleships *Scharnhorst* and *Gneisenau* with his armed merchant cruiser, HMS *Ranpura*. Built by Harland and Wolff in Belfast, she was launched in 1925 and joined the P&O fleet with 307 first class and 288 second class berths. Requisitioned by the Admiralty in August 1939, she was converted with eight 6-inch guns and two 3-inch guns, all of First World War vintage.

The retired Captain Keir, aged 58, was on the Admiralty Reserve List when he was recalled to duty and given command of the *Ranpura*. On encountering the enemy he signalled their location to the Admiralty. Despite being heavily outgunned, rather than surrender as demanded by the Germans, he said: "We'll fight them both, they'll sink us and that will be that, but we will delay their getaway." He then turned the *Ranpura* to engage the enemy more closely, in Nelsonian style. They managed to score one hit on *Scharnhorst* before, within forty minutes, being sunk. Two hundred and thirty-eight men, including Captain Keir, went down with the *Ranpura*. Twenty-seven were rescued by the German ships and 11 were picked up by HMS *Chitrail* – another converted passenger ship. Despite the British effort to intercept them with a fleet of warships, the German ships returned safely to Wilhelmshaven.

Two items were of particular interest to George when he visited Charlotte Houston in her apartment in the new stable block, named 'Troy' after the 1979 Derby winner.

The first was an oil painting of the *Ranpura* flying the white ensign, and the second was a display of medals in a glass-topped container, headed by a Military Cross. Charlotte explained that they were her husband, Colonel James Houston's. George's research revealed that, in 1942 while serving as a Lieutenant in the Scots Guards, he was in command of a platoon of six-pounder anti-tank guns. The battalion was defending a ridge at Bir el Rigel in Libya. After days of intense fighting, the battalion was attacked by armoured columns from the 21st Panzer Division on 13th June. His platoon destroyed five German tanks before it was overrun. Houston was captured but escaped the following night. He re-joined his unit the next day after walking 17 miles across the desert.

Born on the 16th March 1926, Charlotte was the only child of Edward Keir and his wife Dorothy who, under the stage name Doriel Paget, was a singer and actress. Encouraged by Richard Attenborough, a family friend, Charlotte, aged sixteen won the Leverhulme Scholarship to the Royal Academy of Dramatic Art (RADA). In 1944, she made her debut on the London stage in Vera Wheatley's *Scandal at Barchester*.

In the summer of 1945, the young, strikingly beautiful, Charlotte Keir went on stage to perform for the Allied troops in Germany. She never forgot the experience. The 2000 soldiers filling the theatre hoped to watch Charlotte sing and dance in a revue. Already the vivacious, long-legged actress had proved a sensation entertaining Allied forces with Entertainment National Service Association (ENSA) in the Low Countries.

That night, however, realising that Charlotte was to perform in a play, the men marched out. Her audience shrank, Charlotte later observed, to about 90.

It was after one of her ENSA performances that a young army officer, James Houston, approached her; an engagement ring soon followed with the promise that marriage would not put a stop to her career. Her uncle, like her deceased father, a naval Captain, in his wedding speech, commented that the Senior Service welcomed James and the magnificent swirl of the Scots Guards pipes.

James was true to his word and after a stint at Worthing Rep she returned to the West End to sparkle as Cherry in *The Beaux Stratagem*. *The Times* theatre critic remarked that "Miss Charlotte Keir has the same freedom as the landlord's pretty daughter and uses it most takingly". For this, Charlotte won a Clarence Derwent award and her career flourished.

With the arrival of her first child, she decided to devote herself to her family, which rapidly numbered three offspring. She continued to enjoy directing and acting in the regiment's amateur productions, wherever her husband's postings took her.

On James' retirement as a Colonel and with her children now grown up and the arrival of television, she approached her old agency with a view to reactivating her professional career, which she enjoyed with supporting character roles in television productions as diverse as *Z Cars*, *Secret Army*, *Bergerac*, *The Jewel in the Crown*, *Miss Marple* and *Inspector Morse*.

After her husband's death in his 80s, she decided not to be a burden to her two sons and daughter, who were only too happy to accommodate her in a 'Granny Flat', but to be independent. Having visited a now-departed friend at Hinton Court, she thought that the place would be ideal for her.

George and Charlotte met almost daily and he introduced her to The *Times* crossword, which they used to complete together.

With his magic tricks, George was a favourite of Charlotte's grandchildren, and their parents.

Robert Houston, Charlotte's eldest son, the country's leading expert on Elizabethan miniatures became the head of the V&A. Jack Houston made a name for himself as a roadkill chef – deer, pheasant, pigeon – at the Royal Oak, Brockenhurst, in the New Forest.

Charlotte was delighted when her daughter, Fiona Houston, became a renowned actress, who married the actor Sir Malcolm Morton, and became the mother of Henry Morton, who was to become a successful television drama director.

In January 1940, Charles Macfarlane went up to Oxford to read Modern Languages. He took a war-shortened BA and joined the Scots Guards, becoming a close friend of James Houston and, latterly, the Houston family.

In the last days of the war, Lieutenant Macfarlane was travelling in Germany, with his driver and a Sergeant, when his jeep was stopped. A German officer, with tunic insignia indicating a man of rank, had stepped into the road waving a white shirt. Speaking in good English, he said: "I am surrendering my men to you and expect good treatment of them in accordance with the Geneva rules."

Macfarlane replied that they would be well treated; that they must be told to leave all weapons behind. Those would be collected later.

The German then blew a whistle and shouted, in German: "All weapons to be left and then come out." He handed his holstered pistol to Macfarlane as, from the surrounding buildings, over 100 men emerged with their hands held high or on top of their heads. Macfarlane told the German officer to line his men up behind the jeep, and to tell them they could lower their hands, and then he would lead them to a prisoner of war camp.

When the procession arrived at headquarters, Charles's Colonel congratulated him and moved towards his equivalent ranked German. He stopped as he drew near and with a puzzled look said: "Is that you, Gustav?" The German gave an affirmative nod. Shaking him by the hand the Colonel said: "Good to see you after all these years." He then turned and raised his voice to Charles "We were at Cambridge together."

This incident brought relief and smiles to some of the prisoners' faces.

Charles was released from the army in 1946. Through a family friend an introduction was made and he joined the book department of the auctioneer Sotheby's in 1947.

From an early age he had shown an interest in Medieval manuscripts and when he got a scholarship to Eton, he was granted a rarely permitted admission to the college library where he asked to see *The Eton Apocalypse*. This was an illuminated manuscript by Saint John, telling the story of the Apocalypse in the Book of Revelation. Written in Norman French, with

98 illustrations, it was dated between 1250 and 1300. Charles remembered the Provost – M R James, as famous for his chilling ghost stories as his scholarship – "holding it open as far away as he could from me."

At Sotheby's, he eventually became head of the department, setting new scholarly standards, writing the catalogue descriptions himself and, from the rostrum, taking the sales of a range of antique books, fine bindings and manuscripts, which achieved record prices.

In his late 30s, Charles, an expert skier, had met the Russian photographer Svetlana Poliakoff on the slopes of Saint Moritz. They later married and had two daughters and a son. Svetlana was able to see them make happy marriages and produce grandchildren before she died of cancer. Charles was bereft, they had been a devoted pair, sharing a love of art and architecture.

Having visited Charlotte Houston at Hinton Court, Charles decided to move there and pursue a passion he had always had – bookbinding: a craft dating back to the ancient Egyptians and papyrus.

When Hester asked if he would give a talk to the residents about auctioneering at Sotheby's, to her surprise he said he'd rather do an illustrated talk about bookbinding. His unsuspecting audience was soon gripped by his excellent delivery of what was revealed to be a fascinating subject. A shocking example being the disclosure that the skin of executed criminals was sometimes used in 18th century book binding.

CHAPTER 6

On Rosamund Tenant's death, a newspaper article surprised many of the residents at Hinton Court who had fond memories of a kind, amusing, popular widow. It revealed that, in 1945, her father William Burden had been condemned as a traitor and shot by a firing squad.

Unlike Edward VIII and many of the aristocracy and upper classes – as portrayed in Kazuo Ishiguro's *The Remains of the Day* – he was not just a sympathiser of Nazi Germany but became an active supporter: a spy.

In the early 1930s, Burden, who had a history degree from Cambridge and was an accomplished sportsman; he had rowed in the eight which won the University Boat Race in 1929, as well as representing Cambridge in the tennis team. He also successfully raced cars at the Brooklands banked track. A popular teacher at Dulwich College, he was rising to prominence in the British Union of Fascists (BUF).

Rosamund, when interviewed for a biography of her father, remembered him taking her to the BUF HQ in Sloane Square, and showing her the Blackshirt paraphernalia. On the way back home she recalled him singing "*Dulwich over Alice*"; it was only years later that she realised he must have been singing *Deutschland über Alles*.

She had mixed feelings about her father. Though no Nazi sympathiser and no apologist for treachery, she could not help being fond of him and told his biographer how, in the years before the war, he had been a good and attentive parent. "He used to do funny things to make me laugh. He would play the piano and sing silly songs, and take me for boat rides in Battersea Park. He was a lovely father."

Rosamund became a teacher and taught at the co-educational boarding school Bedales, where she met fellow teacher Hugo Tenant. Fully aware of her background, they were married in 1955. He predeceased her after a long and happy union. Their three sons with their families had been frequent visitors to Hinton Court.

The arrival, a week apart, of Richard Leighton and Lady Kedrova, both now single, engendered knowing smiles from other residents when they met and soon became an 'item'. Richard, although very deaf, was deceptively fit and a fast walker. When asked by another male resident to slow down and give his age he astonished his companion by revealing that he was 84 – seven years his senior. Richard became very active in the "joint activities", particularly the Book Club and the Art Group, where his work was much admired.

In 1939, he was at Oxford reading Modern Languages when war broke out, he joined the King's Royal Rifles. In 1944, as a Lieutenant, he served throughout the Italian campaign and experienced the bitter close-quarters fighting at Monte Cassino with the resulting lifeless: staring, open-eyed twisted young bodies.

The dead from both sides were listed from their identity discs before friends and foes were buried with as much dignity as the circumstances allowed.

Even the toughest survivors suffered nightmares for the rest of their lives and there were many unpublicised subsequent suicides engendered by what they had seen and done.

It was at Monte Cassino that Richard was Mentioned in Despatches for, whilst under fire, taking papers from a dead German officer, amongst which was a map showing strategic German defence points.

Badly wounded during a later attack he was thought to have been killed. When he appeared amongst his unit, having dragged himself over a mile, his fellow officers were stunned: "We thought you were dead."

During the advance up the Italian peninsula, Richard had been fascinated by the unspoilt vineyards and had sampled some of their wares. After his recuperation, with the war ended, he decided to tour the wineries of Europe. Through a relative, he received sponsorship from the wine merchants Justerini and Brooks, for whom he made some successful suggestions, and was asked to join them.

In due course he became a Master of Wine and the head of a team of six buyers for The Wine Society. Established in 1874, the Society was created and still operates as a co-operative, with each member owning one share. Because it is owned by and sells only to its members, the buyers are not tasked with meeting specific selling prices and commercial priorities to maximise profits but with finding high-quality, interesting, and value-for-money wines from around the world, at all price levels.

Nicolette Kedrova was the third wife and widow of the shipping tycoon Sir Paolo Kedrova (Knighted for Services to the Arts, he had financed a new wing at the National Gallery) who was known for his impressive collection of three 18/19th century English landscape artists who are now considered by many to have been the inspiration for the French Impressionists. In an age when landscape painting was considered inferior to historical narrative and portrait work, Joseph Turner (1775-1851), Thomas Girtin (1775-1802) and John Constable (1776-1837) came to the fore. On his death, Paolo Kedrova bequeathed his considerable collection to the nation, less works, one by each of the three, that were now with his widow at Hinton Court.

Joseph Turner and Thomas Girtin were students together at Dr Thomas Monro's academy, and remained firm friends during Girtin's short life. It is feasible that they drew or painted portraits of each other. At the time of Girtin's death, both he and Turner were on the threshold of fame. Of the two, Girtin had the greater admiration of their fellow artists, and Turner said: "If Tom Girtin had lived, I should have starved – he was a brilliant fellow."

Nicolette, daughter of the well-known society portrait painter, Owen Watkins-Williams, went to Elmhurst School for Dance and the Performing Arts. Her ambition was to become a dancer but when in her teens she grew to five foot eleven inches, an agent suggested that she became a model. She was an immediate success.

Aged 19 she married the polo-playing Captain Wentworth Fowler, who soon divorced her when it was discovered that she was unable to have children. She then became the trophy wife of millionaire scientist and amateur jockey, John Reed, who rode in the Grand National, finishing the course. But not the marriage course with Nicolette. Their separation and divorce completed, she, now in her thirties, met Paolo Kedrova, twenty years her senior, and they became a devoted couple.

His grown-up children were at first sceptical and distant but soon realised her genuineness. She was not only accepted but given embracing warmth, especially by Paolo's daughter, Melina, who had married a drug addict and had herself become reliant on heroin. When Melina and her husband were found dead together from overdoses, their son Theo, aged two, filled the missing element in Nicolette's life. Grandfather Paolo happily approved her surrogate motherhood and rejoiced to see how, over the years, Theo accepted and returned her love. Now an adult, he was a constant visitor to Hinton Court.

At the Christmas lunch given by Hester for residents and their guests, Paolo's adult children, having met and liked Richard and his daughter Yvonne, a successful potter, were pleased at Nicolette's new relationship and heartily approved when she told them Richard had suggested she join him on a cruise.

The two gave details to their families and the Head Warden who was asked to say that they had both happened to go off to visit relatives at the same time.

The *Noble Caledonia* trip to St. Petersburg was specifically to see the magnificent 'Hermitage' art collection but also to enjoy ballet productions and get a flavour of Russia.

There were those who suggested that the two oldies, set in their individual ways, would soon fall apart when living together in such close proximity (they had booked a double cabin) but quite the contrary happened. It sealed Richard and Nicolette's relationship.

CHAPTER 7

After five years, Hinton Court was well-established and prospering; then two arrivals unwittingly threatened its success. Rory and Flora MacLeod, both in their seventies, decided to sell Manor Farm at Stoke Bissett, on the edge of Salisbury Plain. As none of their three married daughters, or grandchildren, had been interested in taking it on with its 620 acres adjacent to the military training area, they got a good price from the Ministry of Defence, and the Jacobean manor became the officer's mess for a tank regiment.

The MacLeods decided to pay a visit to Hinton Court and their eyes lit up when inspecting the newly available 'Blakeney', named after the 1969 Derby winner.

The MacLeods became a popular couple, the King and Queen of the croquet lawn, but trouble was brewing. On a canal trip organised by the Head Warden, eight of the residents were enjoying the scenery and birdlife when Rory had a stroke. After a brief stay in hospital, he was allowed to return to Hinton Court but he had to go into the nursing home, where he could be easily visited by his wife, and reasonably often by his family. Unfortunately, he developed dementia. His memory deteriorated, he became thoughtless, disorganised, slovenly, confused and cantankerous.

Rory MacLeod was aware he had dementia, for which there is no cure. He knew that he would eventually become hand fed by tube and incontinent, and made it clear that he wanted to die. "I don't want to end up with some poor carer wiping my bottom. I'd rather end my life while I'm still reasonably manageable, and don't want to become a burden and less and less of a person."

There was talk of flying him to the Dignitas clinic in Switzerland, for an "accompanied suicide", but the matron and a carer heard this normally gentle man shouting at his wife and eldest daughter Morag , a consultant at Odstock Hospital, Salisbury, that he wanted to die in England and be a part of the 'Dignity in Dying' campaign. Soon after this outburst he was found one morning dead. He seemed to have died what can best be described as a natural death, in the night.

But Matron was concerned. She decided to have a private talk with Hester. "I'm sorry to say, I think we have had an 'assisted death'. The last person to visit Mr MacLeod was his doctor daughter, Morag. We all know that he wanted to die, but 'assisted death' is still illegal. Do we report a suspicious death?"

Although Hester realised the possibility of bad publicity for Hinton Court, her response was mainly activated by her belief and ardent support of 'Dignity in Dying'. There were many MPs trying to get a Bill through Parliament., often quoting those US states where assisted suicide was legalised. But Hester had read that their legislation was very difficult to enact. In America, you had to be diagnosed with a terminal illness with less than six months to live and be capable of self-administering and ingesting medications without assistance. She hoped that in the UK requirements would be simpler.

Hester and Matron suspected that Morag had given her father a pill. Hester had kept an article from the 'Dignity in Dying' magazine, which she showed to Matron.

> *In general, the law recognises those that assist a loved*
> *one to die under two separate categories; in both*
> *scenarios the law regards their actions as an offence.*
> *First, those who only assist. In other words, their*
> *actions are not the direct cause of death. An example of*
> *this first category might be someone who places the*
> *tablets and water necessary for an overdose before the*
> *deceased but does no more. Those persons would be*
> *guilty of the offence of encouraging or assisting in the*
> *suicide of another contrary to s.2 Suicide Act 1961. A*
> *jury may consider this offence as an alternative to*

murder and manslaughter. This carries a maximum
sentence on indictment of 14 years' imprisonment.
The second category is where the actions of the person went
beyond assistance and proved to be the direct cause of death.
Using the above example of an overdose, the person would
not only provide the tablets and water but administer them
to the deceased with their consent. This might be because
the deceased was too ill to administer them herself. In those
circumstances the law demands a conviction for murder.

Hester had followed some of the cases where relatives were charged and tried. And when the accused had not denied their assistance in the death of a dear one, and expressed the hope that their admission would help others, the juries in a majority of cases had supported them. She produced another article for matron to read.

A judge made the rare step of attacking the Crown
Prosecution Service for pursuing a case of attempted
murder against a loving mother who helped her seri-
ously ill daughter to die.
Stoking the debate over mercy killings, he praised the
common sense, decency and humanity of the jury at
Lewes crown court, who took just two hours to clear
Kay Gilderdale over the death of 31-year-old Lynn.
Kay Gilderdale administered a cocktail of lethal drugs
to end Lynn's life, after her daughter called her for help
when her own attempts at suicide failed.
The jury foreman smiled at Gilderdale as he announced

a unanimous verdict of not guilty, amid applause and weeping in the public gallery.

The 55-year-old mother was prosecuted for attempted murder despite admitting a charge of aiding and abetting the suicide of her bedridden daughter, who had suffered a severe form of MS for 17 years.

The case is the latest involving the prosecution of different mothers who acted in what they saw as a merciful way to end a child's suffering.

But in the case of Frances Inglis last week, an Old Bailey jury convicted her of murder, and the judge, sentencing her to jail, said there was "no concept in law of mercy killing" in this country. A killing was still a killing, he said, "no matter how kind the intention".

At Lewes Mr Justice Bean, the Gilderdale trial judge, openly challenged prosecutors, demanding to know who had made the decision to pursue the case.

"Are you in a position to tell me why it was thought to be in the public interest to proceed with the prosecution of attempted murder rather than accepting the plea of assisted suicide?"

Simon Clements, head of the special crime division, said the decision was made by his team. "The intent was clear, on our evidence,' he said. "We are in the territory of attempted murder. People are not entitled to take the life of another person, however sympathetic one might be of the circumstances, the state of health of the person concerned and all the surrounding circumstances."

He added it would be up to parliament to change the law as it stood.

Gilderdale was charged with attempted murder rather than murder because – toxicology tests could not clarify which of the doses had proved to be fatal – the one Miss Gilderdale administered herself in her attempt to take her life – or the ones given by her mother. Addressing Gilderdale, who had looked after her daughter 24 hours a day since she was struck by a severe form of MS aged 14, the judge said "There is no dispute that you were a caring and loving mother and that you considered that you were acting in the best interests of your daughter."

After a lengthy discussion, Hester proposed, and Matron agreed, that they did not call in Morag and tell her of their suspicions, or report the matter to the police.

They suspected that Flora had agreed to Morag's action, probably with a pill, openly given to Rory, who with gratitude would have swallowed it. That when Hester suggested to Flora that early cremation would be sensible, she would conclude that the nursing home knew what had happened and were taking no action.

CHAPTER 8

W hen Robert and Stephanie Wilson arrived at Hinton Court they were quickly accepted and frequently asked over for drinks by other residents.

On leaving Cambridge University, Robert had started his career in art at the Courtauld Institute, before being called up and spending the Second World War years in the Royal Naval Volunteer Reserve, on the notorious Arctic convoys to Russia. As a Lieutenant, he was Mentioned in Despatches for picking up survivors from torpedoed merchantmen, with German submarines still in the area.

After the war, he re-embarked on his career as an art curator, becoming the first professional art adviser to the Ministry of Works, establishing what has now become the Government Art Collection, which graces many buildings and embassies. He acquired, at modest prices, works by living artists, such as Elizabeth Frink and David Hockney, when they were relatively unknown.

In 1946, he met Stephanie Furness at a dance. She had dazzled so many junior diplomats that she had rejected marriage proposals in four languages, before accepting one from Robert.

In September 1939, aged 19, she was in Moscow, the daughter of Brigadier Furness, Britain's military attaché in Russia. Joseph Stalin, after speaking with Stephanie, remarked to him: "What a clever little dochka (daughter)." There was no doubting her linguistic skills and she returned to London to translate Russian, Swiss, Dutch and French newspapers for military intelligence.

In 1943, she was sent by MI6 to the British Embassy in Istanbul to teach its foreign agents to code. She also ensured they did not leave Istanbul with British luxury items that might betray them, and once confiscated some Harvey Nichols underwear.

On her return to London, she worked with a team of forgers and safecrackers who had been released from prison to work with MI6. They picked locks and steamed wax seals on diplomatic bags that had arrived at London airport (now Heathrow). These reports from heads of state to their embassies would be collected by an MI6 agent disguised as a Foreign Office chauffeur. Wearing white gloves, Stephanie would skim through the contents and photograph relevant documents.

After the war she worked with Robert, sharing a fascination for paintings, buildings and books. Their three children and several grandchildren were frequent visitors to Hinton Court.

In the stable block the door of 'Nimbus', the 1949 Derby winner, was opened from the inside to reveal Stephanie and Robert Wilson standing on the doorstep. "We were near neighbours of Colonel David Vincent and wondered if we could help. I'm Robert Wilson and this is my wife Stephanie. Any stuff you want to get rid of we could take to the skip, near the staff car park."

The woman, in her sixties, who had opened the door, said: "That's kind of you, come in. My name's Joan Weaver and I'm David's daughter – he spoke of you – and I have quite a lot of stuff for the skip but let's have a cup of tea, or would you prefer coffee?"

Stephanie replied that tea would be good and, as they followed her to the kitchen, Robert said: "I'm sorry we missed the funeral, we only got back from staying with our son's family this week and heard what an exceptional event it was. Fly-past by an Auster and helicopter from Middle Wallop. Cap, medals and flying gloves on his coffin, with a bugler blowing not just *The Last Post* but also *Those Magnificent Men in Their Flying Machines*.

"I don't think many, if any, of the residents had a proper knowledge of his achievements. I know the Army has more helicopters than the RAF, but gather he wrote a book: *Flying an Unarmed Auster for the Royal Artillery in the Korean War.*"

Joan explained: "Yes. He got the flying bug as a teenager, from his aunt Mary, who flew with the ATA in the Second World War.

Stephanie looked puzzled "The ATA?"

Joan smiled. "Funnily enough I've just come across her obituary, which dad kept. I'll get it." And to Stephanie: "Will you make the tea?"

While she was out of the kitchen, Robert said: "And I'd like to know what the citation was for his Distinguished Flying Cross – normally associated with the RAF."

Joan returned holding a file and, after the tea was poured, she pulled out a newspaper cutting and explained: "The headline, in heavy print, reads: 'Mary Vincent, one of the first women to fly Spitfires, has died aged 94'. This is followed by 'In a recent interview Mary said that joining the ATA was the best job to have had during the war because it was exciting and we could help the war effort.'

'The all male Air Transport Auxiliary (unofficial motto "Anything to Anywhere") was formed in September 1939 to ferry planes from the factories where they were built to maintenance units for equipment. The pilots were those who had been excluded from the RAF as too old. Once the Phoney War burst into reality in the summer of 1940, the work of the ATA became a priority and the call went out for women flyers. Mary told how in January 1943 she had broken through thick cloud in a Spitfire she was delivering, banked sharply to avoid a patch of woodland and landed in heavy rain on the grass airstrip of the Navigation and Blind Flying Establishment at RAF Windrush and that "An RAF man sloshed towards me with a rain cape and said 'I say miss, you must be good on instruments'. To his astonishment I showed him my handheld compass and said 'This is my only instrument, my other aids being a watch and a map.' We ATA pilots flew unarmed, without radios, never mind instruments. If a Messerschmitt 109 blasted out of the sun we were toast'.

'Of the 168 female pilots in the ATA, 15 were killed. These included the famous Amy Johnson, who bailed out of her Airspeed Oxford over the Thames Estuary. Her body was never found.

Let us remember with gratitude the men and women of the Air Transport Auxiliary, whose astonishing achievements deserve to be better known."

Joan looked up and smiled as Robert exhaled "Phew!" and said: "So David was a chip off the old block and got a DFC for flying an Auster in Korea?"

Joan answered "My father explains in his book that because of the mountain terrain in Korea, an air observation flight was vital, and he was one of the six Royal Artillery pilots who flew five Austers, supported by around forty RAF technicians. Their prime tasks were to spot enemy positions, direct artillery, and provide photographic reconnaissance. Although UN had air superiority they had to face anti-aircraft fire; two pilots were killed and two shot down and captured."

She put the cutting back in the file and pulled out an official-looking piece of paper. "I thought you might be interested; here's the citation for his DFC."

Robert glanced at it, gave a look to Stephanie, and turned back to read aloud:

"Captain David Vincent RA came to Korea with this Flight in July 1951 and has been flying continuously on operations since that time.

Throughout the period his efficiency, zeal and devotion to duty have been of a very high order. He has conducted a very large number of shoots with both Divisional and Corps artillery with great success and in so doing has been personally responsible for inflicting considerable damage upon the enemy.

Many of these shoots have been against heavily dug in enemy gun positions well behind the front lines. Successful engagement of these by precision adjustments on to each gun pit calls for steady flying deep into enemy territory for two hours at a time. On the very frequent occasions he has carried out these tasks, Captain Vincent has consistently displayed coolness and deter-mination and, even in the face of enemy AA has allowed nothing to deter him from completing his allotted task for the sortie.

On one occasion last November he was carrying out a dusk sortie and a considerable number of enemy guns opened fire inflicting casualties on our troops. As things turned out this proved to be the preliminary bombard-ment to a heavy infantry attack. Captain Vincent flew deep into enemy territory and pin pointed no less than

27 active gun positions in the fading light. His action in this instance enabled our artillery to retaliate with quick and effective counter battery fire and so be of considerable assistance to our own heavily pressed infantry.

Quiet efficiency, zeal for the task in hand and great determination have characterised this officer's work consistently and I recommend his excellent services are recognised by an appropriate award.

"It's signed by his Commanding Officer and countersigned by the Brigade Commander, the General Officer commanding the 1st Commonwealth Division, and two Commanders in Chief."

CHAPTER 9

The artist and critic Alastair Robertson, who had died aged 82, was known to have worn very lightly his title as the 6th Marquess of Inverness, which came to him in 1981 when he was 63, on the death of his elder brother Archie. It did not change his mischievous ways, particularly his enjoyment of shocking the stuffy establishment by writing repeatedly of his experiences in the fashionable bordellos of Knightsbridge and the Middle East. A year before his death, *The Oldie* magazine printed an article entitled *The Good Whore Guide*, in which he reported his experiences as a 'sex starved subaltern' with Irina, an Albanian girl in Mme Coral's establishment in Beirut in 1942.

In 1948, Alastair married the ceramics sculptor Anne Carey, who built up a thriving business as a creator of figurines and decorated their home with her colourful flocks of ceramic parrots. She produced two daughters and a son who became the 7th

Marquess. Anne, a strong, handsome character, was a lively and generous hostess, known to point out that she was the breadwinner in the partnership. Now the Dowager Marchioness of Inverness, she thought it best to move out of the ancestral home and wrote to Hinton Court saying that she'd like to visit with a view to moving in but needed accommodation that would take her ceramics equipment. When shown 'Hyperion', named after the Derby winner of 1933, she immediately said: "I'll take it." Soon after, having settled in and reactivated her kiln, Hester asked if she would like to give a 'talk' on her work in the drawing room – a screen could be erected to show examples. Anne, who had quickly become a popular resident, accepted the invitation and proved an excellent speaker and demonstrator. As with authors who sold their books after their talks, her display of ceramics for sale was soon scooped up by an enthusiastic audience.

There was another important element in her life, heightened when she became a Marchioness – voluntary public service and a strong sense of duty. In her case it had been encapsulated by her parents who were both involved in the National Society for the Prevention of Cruelty to Children (NSPCC), founded by the Reverend Benjamin Waugh (1839-1908). Anne used her charm to cajole or just command people to part with their money. Her belief in the cause and her obvious love of children egged them on to give just that bit more.

A natural speaker, she never missed an opportunity to talk about the NSPCC and encourage support for it. Her trenchant views and common sense were often expressed when faced with ideas which she felt were not focused on the best interest of the children. She had known many of the front-line protection officers personally and understood the complications and stresses of their work.

≈

Moira Carpenter was sometimes asked why she had come to Hinton Court and not returned to her birthplace, Scotland, for her final years. She explained that her late husband was English, and although she had grown up with the future Marquis of Inverness, Alastair Robertson, as a neighbour, when she had visited his widow, Anne, now deceased, at Hinton Court she had been impressed by its ambience.

On Moira's arrival there was something about her that rang a bell and instigated efforts among the residents to unearth who she was. Her background was revealed when two of them, simultaneously, discovered she had had a privileged, but at the same time deprived upper-class childhood in a Scottish castle, educated by governesses.

During the second world war, having started as an aircraft fitter working on heavy bombers, she became a technical advisor at the Ministry of Production. Moira Grant married Captain John Carpenter, Royal Artillery, in 1943 and they had two daughters.

Moira Carpenter was the author of *Peddle Power:*

From the Atlantic to the Pacific, a journey of nearly 5000 miles across the USA on an ordinary bicycle. Its rider Moira, in her late fifties and a grandmother, who normally just used her bicycle for shopping, did no special preparation. "If I had taken extra exercise I would have found that some bits of me ached so badly that I would have been put off the idea."

Her next book, *The Ghosts Were Friendly*, describes aspects of her education, or rather lack of it: *The castle teemed with historical records; books, furnishings and objets d'art of every kind that could have been used to capture our imagination, but nobody drew our attention to them and we remained totally unconscious both of them and the ancestry that had led, through nearly a thousand years of recorded genealogy, to our own births.*

Her brilliant opening of the book began:

When I was a little girl, the ghosts were more real to me than the people. The people were despotic and changeable, governing my world with a confusing and alarming inconsistency. The ghosts, on the other hand, could be relied on to go about their haunting in a calm and orderly manner. Bearded or bewigged, clad in satin or velvet or nunlike drapery, they whispered their way along the dark corridors of the castle where I was born and spent the first ten years of my life, rarely interfering with or intruding on the lives of the living.
My mother couldn't understand why the servants were frightened of the ghosts. Sitting in the sunny bow window of the Big Drawing Room, she would watch yet another maid – scanty possessions stuffed into a

*carpet-bag – fleeing down the drive that led through the
towering beech trees to the main road, and murmur
sadly.*

*"I can never get them to understand that the ghosts
won't* hurt *them. If only they'd just ask the poor things
what they* want."

*It was dinned into us that if we found ourselves face to
face with a ghost we must ask it what it wanted.*

*"They only haunt because they're worried, poor
things," my mother would explain in her soft voice,
"Ask them if there is anything you can* do *for them.
And for goodness' sake don't be frightened. After all,
they're all your ancestors – whatever is there to be
frightened of?"*

*So, as a child, I was never scared of the ghosts. But I
didn't go out of my way to meet them, either. I respected
their privacy, and they mine.*

*There were four chief ghosts in the castle. The quietest
was an old man in a velvet coat, who used to sit
reading in the library; he was so peaceful that one could
be in the room for several minutes without even noticing
that he was there, but as soon as one did notice he
would softly vanish, fading into the leather upholstery.
The woman in a long grey dress was just as untrouble-
some; her face half covered with a sort of bandage
similar to that worn by some orders of nuns, she would
come through the wall-cupboard of the nursery and
bend over the babies in their cradles, like a nurse
checking to see if her charges were sleeping peacefully.
Equally unobtrusive was the woman who regularly
crossed one of the upper rooms of the tower (built in*

1210) and vanished into a loft; her only fault was that she did not know that since her time the room had been converted into a bathroom, and her sudden appearance sometimes unnerved male guests who, surprised in the bath, were almost relieved to discover that the woman who had entered was only a spectre. Far from quiet, however, was the red-haired young man on the stairs. He was a ghost who loved parties, and he could be relied on to turn up whenever there was festivity. Ceremonial evening dress for men having changed hardly at all for at least a hundred years, his appearance in kilt, sporran trimmed with ermine-tails, lace-edged shirt and silver-buttoned jacket, excited no particular comment among the merrymakers. It was only when some elderly woman guest would petulantly ask my mother to tell "the young man with the red beard" not to push past people on the stairs that my mother would know that he was out again. But anyone who slept in the tower could hear him on non-party nights as well, laughing and joking with his friends as he ran lightly up and down the steep spiral stairs. Often, after I was promoted from the nursery to a room in the tower, I would lie awake in the dark, with the blankets pulled high under my chin, listening to the ghosts. But I never could make out what it was that they said.

Moira became a leading light in the book club, joined art classes and became known as a fearsome bridge player.

CHAPTER 10

The widowed actress Aimée de Caux OBE (for Services to Drama) had opted not to end up in the 'Actor's Retirement Home', where she said there would be continuous competition for who had had the best parts and unending theatrical talk. Another possible reason (not voiced) was that there might be those who knew about her background. Although there were a surprising number of actors, like Charles Dance, who were known to have come from a humble background, but were unashamed and amused to find themselves often type-cast as aristocrats, Aimée did not want her cover blown.

Ethel Binks was a tall and striking 17 year old, working as a housemaid at the Grand Hotel, Norwich, when spotted by a theatrical agent and asked if she had considered being a model or actress. As Ethel had recently been praised by a visiting drama adjudicator to her school for her Eliza Doolittle in Shaw's

Pygmalion, and had always dreamed of being in the 'movies', she said "an actress".

Dawn Stockwell, the agent, said: "Well, I'll invest in you – no point in trying to get into RADA, Central or other stage schools. I'll pay for elocution and dance lessons to get rid of your Norfolk accent and improve your deportment. But first we'll have to change your name." Having been brought up in Bramwell Castle in Norfolk, a daughter of the chauffeur and a house-maid, Ethel had absorbed the place's history and the stories behind the pictures. The early owners of the castle were the now-extinct de Cauxs, who arrived with William the Conqueror, and her hero was Henry de Caux, who had fought at the battle of Agincourt. She could never pass Holbein's sepia drawing of Lady Aimée de Caux without 'communing' with her. A court beauty, she had caught Henry VIII's eye before Anne Boleyn. When Ethel Binks now suggested that she became Aimée de Caux, Dawn raised an eyebrow, smiled, and said "brilliant".

Aimée started as a film extra and was soon noticed by various directors, given a line or two of dialogue and, like Audrey Hepburn, who started similarly, was groomed for stardom, becoming one of Pinewood's "Glamour Girls". Dawn, with her 10% of fees, soon recouped her investment. She tried, unsuccessfully, to stop Aimée's first marriage, pointing out that it would deter her fans. Though successful in her work she became well known for her many liaisons and was married three times. She had one child, a daughter, Nadia, by Warren Wesley, a Hollywood "heart throb".

A promising young actress, Nadia was killed whilst involved in a filmed car chase which went horribly wrong.

Aimée became self-educated in the theatrical world, researching the descriptions of popular productions and how famous names had interpreted various roles on the stage, as well as the screen. She listened to recordings, watched films and surprised friends with her intelligent contributions when relevant performances came up for discussion.

She was not as well known as some of her contemporaries, but was often booked for television parts when they were not available. When asked how she felt about being second choice so often, she quoted her friend, Fay Compton: "We are all thirteenth choice, dear," and would recount how, when none of the big names were available to play Henry VIII in the 1970s series *The Six Wives of Henry VIII*, at the last moment before filming started, the Australian actor Keith Michell was cast – and was magnificent.

Ironically, the principal at RADA asked Aimée to join his teaching staff. She described the time there as one of the most stimulating and rewarding periods of her life.

With her height and aristocratic bearing she was totally convincing in her last role, playing a guest duchess in the TV series *Downton Abbey*. Her one scene with the dowager Duchess of Grantham (Maggie Smith) was so amusing and captivating that she became a semi-regular, with their scenes, which were much anticipated and enjoyed, getting deserved acclaim in the 'audience reports'.

The resident responsible for recommending Hinton Court to Aimée was the much-admired retired television drama director Herbert Harrison. She had worked for him many times and they had a platonic mutual admiration. One of her favourite roles was as Calphurnia, the wife of Julius Caesar, in his still-remembered series *The Caesars*. She exclaimed "snap" and told him of her name change, after he had told her his original name.

Heini Rosenbaum was born in Vienna in 1926 and, aged 12, was rescued from the Nazi occupation by the Kindertransport. Despite being unable to speak English, he was welcomed by a childless couple, the Harrisons, who lived in Preston, Lancashire. They treated him as their son and, on hearing that both his parents had died in the Treblinka extermination camp, officially adopted Heini, who had already been re-named Herbert Harrison.

The boy soon settled in, quickly acquiring a Northern English accent, doing well at school and, in his late teens, he became determined to contribute to the war effort. His ambition was to become a pilot and he applied to join the RAF but, after a good interview, was discovered to be colour-blind, and instead of flying, was asked to work in Intelligence.

In 1947 he got into the Birmingham School of

Speech and Drama, and joined the Oldham Repertory Theatre as an actor in 1950, making his directorial debut in Scarborough in 1954. Commercial television arrived in 1956 and he was placed on a training course set up by Granada, establishing himself as a director in the drama department with his successful *Have You Reached Your Verdict?*, a series of unscripted trials for which the writers gave each actor a backstory for their character but left the rest for improvisation.

In 1962 he was with the BBC, directing *Z Cars*, a powerhouse of experimentation. After Harrison directed the BBC's Civil War drama *The Siege of Corfe Castle* in 1965, the future notoriously obsessive and demanding director Stanley Kubrick (*Spartacus, 2001: A Space Odyssey: Full Metal Jacket*) requested a copy, hoping to learn how to get such strong performances from actors.

One of the aspects of production Harrison enjoyed was choosing music for the opening and closing titles and, where necessary, to enhance scenes. Nowadays, nearly all drama programmes employ a composer. At that time the director relied on the lingeringly named Gramophone Library staff and friends for suggestions allied to his or her own thoughts. As a boy, Herbert had shown talent as a violinist and had a wide knowledge of classical music, as well as jazz in the style of Dave Brubeck.

Cherished by actors and a great innovator, he helped to forge television drama that made it exciting in the 1960s and 1970s. In particular, it was the 12 episodes of *The Caesars* (1976), commissioned to mark BBC Television's 40th anniversary, which grabbed millions with its brutality, decadence and depravity.

Sadly, with a few exceptions, most of his subsequent work was in long-running series. After working on the police series *The Bill*, then past its heyday, and when he was no longer being given a free rein with casting (one of the skills he was celebrated for) he decided to retire and write. He was excited when he signed an option with a film company. The eventual production, of his adaptation of Crosbie Garstein's *The Owl's House*, set in 18th century Cornwall, was well-received.

After his wife, the actress May Mortimer, died, he moved to Hinton Court.

When Herbert heard the beautiful piano sounds of Mendelssohn's *Songs Without Words* being played by his newly-arrived neighbour, he waited until the music had finished, then rang the bell and introduced himself to Katherine Ferguson. He explained that he played the violin – not to her standard – but would be grateful if she would try a duet with him. Katherine suggested he go and get his violin and she would find a Telemann sonata for which she had got the score. Could he sight read? The answer was "yes" and, if it was Sonata No. 4, he knew it. It was.

After going through the piece a couple of times, and making a few suggestions, she said she would be delighted to play with him. So every Thursday from 10:30 they played, with a coffee break, until 12:15, as residents were asked to be seated for lunch at 12:30.

From an early age Katherine Samson had shown talent as a pianist and had emerged from the Royal Academy of Music as one of three getting a distinction with their degrees. The suggestion, not just from her main teacher but also from all the staff with whom she'd been involved, was that she become a concert soloist. She, however, felt that she hadn't a sufficient spread of fingers to cover some chords and settled for being a sought-after accompanist and teacher.

At the age of 23 she became Katherine Ferguson, the wife of a housemaster, 14 years her senior, at Chichester College, where she continued teaching and playing with the city's musical societies; mostly chamber music, but some solo concertos on piano and harpsichord.

A happy life ensued. Her four children completed their time at university, got good jobs, married and started families. Then tragedy struck. Katherine and her husband were travelling in France. When their car was stationary at a crossing a lorry crashed into them. The injuries they sustained killed her husband and she had a back injury that affected her for the rest of her life. With the backing of her family she decided to move to Hinton Court, taking her beloved rare piano, the small but excellent Steck, with her.

When it was suggested by Aimée de Caux that Katherine and Herbert should give a concert, he demurred, saying that whilst she was certainly good enough, he wasn't. But alongside her on the piano he would like to give readings, especially about composers; for example Mendelssohn, of whom Queen Victoria was a fan and wrote eloquently, interposed with relevant pieces played by Katherine. As she did not like the grand piano in the drawing room it was arranged for her Steck to be moved there and tuned before the concert.

After hours spent selecting, putting the music and readings together, and limiting the programme to 50 minutes, it consisted of works by Handel, Bach, Beethoven, Schubert, Mendelssohn, Schumann, Tchaikovsky, and Debussy, interspersed with extracts by Thomas Gray, Wendy Cope, Charles Grove, Queen Victoria, Thomas Hardy, Chaucer, Matthew Arnold, and ending with Daisy Ashford's *A Proposale*.

A packed audience of residents, their families and staff were most appreciative.

CHAPTER 11

The arrival of Venetia Wall with her bicycle raised some smiles, but to many it had not been a surprise, as she had often cycled to Hinton Court to see her friend Moira Carpenter. A few years back she had been commissioned to photograph Moira, with her bicycle, for the front of *Peddle Power, from the Atlantic to the Pacific,* and bicycles had, so to speak, tandemed them together.

Venetia had been a regular sight peddling round Salisbury in Edwardian clothes with a large hat, and did not mind being regarded as an eccentric; indeed she thought the word flattering.

Iris Murdoch and her husband, John Bailey, frequently stayed with Venetia and her family, and Iris wrote a short preface to *Faces*, a book of Venetia's photographs compiled by her son Caspar.

The human face, that complex and significant surface, is the camera's most challenging theme. Venetia Wall's

*remarkable collection of portraits covers the period when
she and her husband, the engraver and painter Howard
Wall, lived at the Old Rectory, Coombe, in Wiltshire.
They were perfect hosts, and their beautiful house and
huge wild garden provided a place of rest and inspiration for their friends, many of whom came to stay and
work there.*

*Solitary concentration or social diversion were both
freely available in that uniquely benign and generous
scene. Venetia, descendent of Elizabeth Fry, bishop's
daughter, singer, developed her talent as a photographer,
particularly a portrait photographer, after her marriage,
when she took to photographing her visiting friends. She
later became a professional; her work is in the perma-
nent collection at the National Portrait Gallery, she has
exhibited at the Royal College of Art and in other
galleries, and includes the Duke of Edinburgh among
her sitters.*

*Venetia's visitors often met and knew each other, but
without ever constituting a 'set'. A number of Blooms-
bury faces make their appearance (for instance
Leonard Woolf, Duncan Grant, Frances Partridge,
Quentin Bell), but the visitors came from many
'worlds'. To list a few of the owners of these interesting faces: Kenneth Clark, Julian Huxley, Benjamin
Britten, Lord David Cecil, Henry Moore, Joyce Gren-
fell, L P Hartley, John Piper, John Betjeman. In this
book of friendship one face, a beautiful one, is absent,
that of Venetia, who has preferred to stay behind the
camera.*

When interviewed for the *Times* magazine she was quoted:

When I was very young I was given a Brownie and I used to send the films off to Lightning Photographic of Torquay. They kept every single thing – they'd got a file which I never knew about until Iris and John Bailey drove us to Torquay once and they said, "Are you really Venetia Wall, née Forest? Would you like to see your file?" And there it was – me from twelve onwards! It was always the face that intrigued me. I was particularly keen on profiles. But it was really only when friends started demanding dust jacket pictures that I decided to make a thing of it. Then publishers began asking me to go and photograph people who'd never met or heard of me. I had three different cameras – a Canon, a Yashica and a wonderful old square Rolleiflex; they were all loaded and my great idea, because I think the face sets the minute people see a camera coming, was to start talking to get their minds off the subject and then take out the different cameras at different places in the room. The whole thing was over in twenty minutes, and it was far better than posing them at great length.

I adored the contrast between, say, Lady Chichester in her siren suit and Henry Moore and his sweet sort of un-grandness. The greater they were the nicer, of course. And the friendlier. But I minded very much when people said, "Look here, I'd rather be smiling," or whatever, and it was an enormous help to have Howard say, "Well, I think that's a frightfully good

*photograph — nothing wrong with that." And that's
really one of the reasons I've been unable to take
photographs since he died — the wish to do it went out
of me when he was no longer there, and I could not
bear to stay in the surrounding we had created and
loved so much together.*

*I originally left home to study at the Royal College of
Music to be a soprano. I walked to the college every day
— I walked everywhere to save money — and of course I
found it all electrifying. The people who took me up
there were Herbert Howells and Vaughan Williams. I
went down to see Vaughan Williams at his house once
or twice, and Herbert Howells came and played the
organ at my wedding. I sang right up to the time I got
married. The singing career was hotting up when I met
Howard but it never occurred to me to go on with it
once I was married, partly because I hadn't got very far
and partly because I thought looking after him was an
infinitely better job —not that I thought of it as a job,
but as a thing I wanted to do.*

The Oldie's review of Caspar Wall's memoir of his
father began:

*Even if Howard Wall is not a name you're familiar
with, you might well recognise his hand:the coat of
arms on a British passport; postage stamps; bank notes
the London Library bookplate; the masthead for the*
Times, *these are just some examples of the vast body
of work produced by Howard, a wood-engraver,
designer, letter-cutter and watercolourist.*

At the Old Rectory his wife Venetia perfected the art of hospitality. Friends enjoyed bedroom fires, breakfast trays, hand-churned butter from her cow, picnics and swimming expeditions. But if Venetia was the ringmaster, the organiser of treats and entertainment, Howard provided intellectual ballast and a still, calm centre. He would work, at one end of the sitting room, serenely oblivious to the people and chat swirling around him.

Extracts from the memoir:

My mother freed my father to get on with his work, untroubled by domestic considerations. She was a different kettle of fish, capricious, lively, funny, impatient, highly strung and a mass of contradictions, outwardly formidable but inside a bundle of nerves. Their opposite natures needed each other. Howard always knew about my mother's liaison with Kenneth ("Civilisation") Clark, which was to last over forty years, and never seemed to bother him. He was secure in the knowledge that his wife loved him and was curiously proud of her love for Clark, whom he admired. He may have been unconsciously aware that Clark filled a gap that he, an artist obsessively wrapped up in his work, couldn't fulfil. Furthermore Clark himself admired Howard's work. Venetia's relationship with Clark was largely conducted on paper, to whom he wrote 1500 letters. Living in the depths of the countryside she found letter-writing her lifeline.
For us children it was she rather than our father who gave us practical guidance as we grew up. However,

*without my father's intellectual gifts, the Old Rectory's
reputation as a paradise of peace and beauty over
which my mother exercised her idiosyncratic imaginative
ideas for entertaining her guests, would never have been
so alluring.*

Once Venetia Wall was well settled into 'Nash-wan', named after the 1989 Derby winner, Hester asked her, and she accepted, to give an illustrated talk with some of her portraits, of the famous people she had taken with her camera - revealing their views on life and their foibles, A rapt audience was soon brought together, its responses peppered with bouts of ecstatic laughter.

CHAPTER 12

The Cavendish Hotel in London was the
hunting ground for some famous *femmes
fatales*, among them was Susan Shelley, who
in the early days of World War II came under the
wing of its famous owner Rosa Lewis (1867-1952).
Daphne Fielding wrote in *The Duchess of Jermyn Street*:

> *Born in Leyton, Rosa maintained her cockney accent,
> wit and high spirits throughout her life. She looked like
> a Queen and swore like a cook, which indeed she was,
> having started as an under-kitchen maid scrubbing
> kitchen floors, aged sixteen, in a grand house.*
> *One evening the Prince of Wales came to dinner and
> afterwards a sing-song was suggested, but a leader was
> lacking. Then the hostess said "There's a girl in the
> kitchen who is always singing. I'll ask her up. She's got
> a good strong voice". "Oh yes, I can sing loud enough,"
> said Rosa, "but I'm not always in tune." And without
> a trace of coyness she led off, and they followed her.*

Afterwards she was presented to the Prince, who complimented her on the excellence of the ptarmigan pie. She dropped a curtsey and laughed as she said "The chef makes the pies, sir, I just take the innards out of the birds sir." Whereupon the Prince patted her on the shoulder and gave her a sovereign.

Rosa never denied rumours that she became the mistress of Edward VII. There is no evidence that she had been but then Rosa, who disapproved of the habit of keeping love letters, would say "No letters, no lawyers and kiss my baby's bottom."

In 1902 she took over the Cavendish Hotel. Her stately carriage and dignified appearance soon earned her the nickname 'The Duchess of Jermyn Street'. In Robin Hood fashion, she charged the poor no more than a nominal sum, and added the rest of their bills to those of the rich. Her calculations a shrewd assessment of willingness and capability, she made sure that no party was given at The Cavendish without her being the principal guest, thus deriving the dual benefit of being paid for the champagne and being its chief consumer. "If you can't have your cake and eat it," she would say, "you can have your champagne and drink it." Nothing could daunt her and when, in 1943, a bomb damaged the hotel, and a part of the ceiling came down on top of her, her first words were "Well the … … didn't get the champagne."

The Cavendish, replete with grand but battered furniture, was a sort of faded country house extension in the heart of the West End, to return to for "extramural activities" after time spent at 'The Gargoyle', which leavened aristocracy with the arts.

Founded in 1925, the rooftop club above Meard Street in Soho was the epitome of decadent glamour. It could only be reached by a small ancient lift, so that strangers left as intimate friends at the top. The interior walls were adorned with mirrors. Members included Noel Coward, Augustus John, Tallulah Bankhead, various Earls and Marquesses, and the spies Guy Burgess and Donald Maclean. The low lighting helped to give it a louche atmosphere. The film-maker Michael Luke described the ambience as: "Mystery suffused with a tender eroticism."

Something of a snob, Rosa was given the impression by Susan Shelley that she came from a "suitable" background. Her father, a "Major in the Guards", had been killed at Ypres, her mother came from a grand family in Galway, Ireland and her great aunt survived the wreckage of the Titanic and was commended for her bravery in saving many children and singing hymns as they rowed to safety. So when Susan brought back a man, or met a man at The Cavendish, it was "alright".

In fact her father was a grocer's assistant and her mother was a seamstress.

Aged sixteen, Susan Shelley modelled in a Newbury dress shop, began an affair with the wealthy husband of a customer and had her first abortion.

She moved to London where she used her beautiful body to model for Schiaparelli, and it was a well-known society photographer who took her for her first visit to the Cavendish.

Rosa would introduce guests to each other and liked to see the young enjoying themselves. The champagne flowed. Susan fitted in perfectly with her good looks and liveliness. During the war people from all walks of life rubbed along and helped each other. They were out for whatever thrills and enjoyment they could get before they were bombed, or sent off to the battlefield. Susan met Kirk, a young Canadian naval officer, who wrote from his ship:

"Every time I've thought of you not staying at the Cavendish today I thanked the Lord. Believe it or not I've always gone there as a single man and I had never realised before what a lecherous establishment it is. I'm really very sorry I persuaded you to come there, although to me our stay was heaven. Two weeks ago I'd have given anything to get home but since you bewitched me it is the last thing I want to do. The idea of leaving you and England seems unbearable now."

But he had to leave quite soon, under orders, "maintaining Britain's lifeline" (his inverted commas). Whilst on that service he died: his ship was torpedoed in the Atlantic and he went down with her.

Some women are different things to many men but Susan Shelley seemed to be the same with them all. At first sight she was kittenish, amusingly troublesome, irresistibly attractive. Later it would emerge what a challenging woman she was; agreeable only when she was in the mood: the victim of incurable boredom which fostered her promiscuity. She extended affections to various writers and a policeman, reflecting that "sex is a great leveller". There was even a lesbian encounter one bored afternoon.

"I just saw her as another man, with breasts."

When she was introduced to the corpulent and unappealing looking Henry Hawes, the great literary stylist, founder and editor of *Vista* (a monthly review of literature and art) he became the love of her life.

They were married in 1950, but after a turbulent five years it ended in divorce, with the publisher William Weiner cited as the co-respondent. He became her second husband, a marriage which would also end in divorce, with Henry Hawes this time cited as co-respondent.

In 1958 she was living with Lord Anstey, who she had met and bedded in The Cavendish war years. They had one of their numerous rows. Inflamed by drink, and after he started hitting her, she grabbed a carving knife to defend herself; they tussled and the knife became embedded in his chest. She immediately called an ambulance and he was rushed to hospital. The police were by his bedside when he became conscious and woozily said: "I was afraid that she wanted to kill me." Susan was charged with attempted murder and remanded in custody to Holloway prison.

At the Winchester trial three months later, which Lord Anstey was able to attend as a witness, he said.

"We were both drunk and I was being violent, she picked up a knife to threaten me and stop me attacking her. It was my fault that in the ensuing struggle the knife entered my body."

In his summing-up the judge pointed out:

"It is quite obvious that Lord Anstey does not wish this woman to be convicted of any offence at all. You may think that the approach to this case is perhaps to negate the intent to murder and the intent to do grievous bodily harm, and confine your attention more to the third charge (that of unlawfully and maliciously wounding). Ask yourselves whether that charge has been made out to your satisfaction."

The jury retired. After 35 minutes the foreman returned to ask the judge if, to find Susan guilty of malicious wounding, they had to be satisfied she intended to frighten. Mr Justice Bracken replied that no element of intent was necessary. They must be satisfied that she knew Lord Anstey was close at hand and that she had deliberately held the knife in his direction.

The jury reached its verdict after another hour and twenty minutes. Not guilty of intent to murder. Not guilty of intent to cause grievous bodily harm. Guilty of unlawful and malicious wounding.

Susan Shelley was sentenced to six months' imprisonment.

Diana Weston, a long-time resident at Hinton Court, had been a prison visitor and had struck up an understanding friendship with Susan Shelley; a relationship which flourished when the latter left prison. Diana suggested that Susan write her memoirs, which she duly did, and then Diana found a publisher for *Crocodile Tears*, whose 'reader' assessed it as: *A comic and sometimes cruel chronicling of her wartime escapades. With a devil-may-care tone, she is unsparing of the famous friends and enemies she made and is certainly not romantic about herself. Her witty rendering of Henry Hawes as a 'great bizarre type' is masterful. Alternatively depressing and very funny, this is an engaging literary achievement.* The book sold well.

Having visited Diana at Hinton Court, Susan wanted to leave her flat in the King's Road, Chelsea, and move into one of the stable apartments, nearby. The word got round that there was the possibility of Susan Shelley joining the community. Some were shocked, they remembered the extensive press coverage of her trial, detailing her very loose lifestyle. Some had frequently raised their eyebrows when reading *Crocodile Tears*.

Hester was approached to stop her coming. She had already been informed of the possibility of objections but Diana offered to be a warranty for Susan's behaviour and, being much respected and liked, she went round assuring those doubters that Susan Shelley would fit in and be a popular asset. Some of them had arrived at Hinton Court depressed after the death of a life partner, with their offspring grown up and often living "across the pond" or in the antipodes, and finding it difficult to leave their home of many decades. Diana was brilliant at helping newcomers adapt to their new lifestyle.

When he had been approached about stopping the arrival of Susan Shelley, Colonel Robert (Bob) Burke gave an enigmatic smile and said: "She would certainly liven up the scene." To Diana Weston he confided: "I have fond memories of Susan Shelley whom I met at the – somewhat notorious – Cavendish Hotel in 1940. She was great fun." Then, with a laugh: "Regretfully we never shared a bed."

On arrival, she was greeted by Hester, Diana, and Bob. She embraced Bob, and turning to Hester and Diana said "Bob and I will have many happy hours reminiscing about Rosa Lewis and the interesting wartime habitués of the Cavendish Hotel," which they did.

The lively Susan Shelley became a welcome 'character', initiating much laughter with the men, as well as the women, at the lunch tables.

By a quirk of fate, the ex-prisoner, Susan Shelley and the one-time prison visitor, Diana Weston, were reunited at Hinton Court with a widowed prison governor, who had been pertinent in both their lives.

When Susan moved from Holloway to an open prison, Hill Hall at Theydon Mount in Essex, Diana continued to visit her. Susan told her that she was impressed by the governor, Dr Rose Johnstone, who was firm but fair and understanding.

On meeting the governor in her office, Diana immediately recognised the head girl from her old school. They were pleased to see each other again and had a good conversation

After Susan's release the years rolled by and, although contact was lost, both Susan and Diana followed Dr Rose Johnstone's career.

In 1946 she had been appointed Assistant Medical Officer in Holloway. Up until then, all medical officers in women's prisons had been men. In 1954, she became governor of the new women's open prison, Hill Hall and later, after Susan had left, Rose was appointed the first female Governor of Holloway, becoming one of the most influential prison administrators of the post-war years. She believed that: "Prisoners should be given hope that they could reform; that by building their self-esteem they could leave prison better prepared for life outside than when they were sentenced." Most importantly she allowed them to keep their babies with them after they had given birth in the prison hospital, as well as allowing them to wear their own clothes and make-up.

She also introduced a variety of classes, covering not just home nursing, first aid, knitting and typing, but gardening, drama and current affairs.

Rose Johnstone became a "go to" for the media, appearing in the papers with her children; pointing out that she, as a married woman with children, had a good understanding of the prisoners, as most of them were also mothers.

Her final appointment was as Director and Inspector of Prisons for Women, making sure that high standards were kept in the women's prisons and borstals throughout England and Wales. She was also a frequent lecturer at the Prison Staff Training College at Wakefield.

After Rose's husband's death Diana met her by chance and asked her down to Hinton Court for lunch and to meet Susan. The trio had plenty to talk about. Although now retired and in her eighties Rose was still a good judge of people and, when introduced, was so impressed by Hester and the atmosphere at Hinton Court that she asked what was available for a 'Lifetime Residency'.

Having moved in, she continued to be a tower of strength to her children, grandchildren, and great grandchildren.

The tranquil routine at Hinton Court would occasionally be enlivened by the visits of television crews to interview Dr Rose Johnstone about relevant events and her extraordinary career.

CHAPTER 13

Bob Burke had been a crack shot at Bisley and on country 'shoots', with his matched pair of Purdey 12 bores. He still spent time on the continent skiing – having represented not just his regiment, the Coldstream Guards, but also the Army.

In 1942, having just arrived in North Africa, Lieutenant Burke used his initiative and with his troops occupied a high vantage point. He was then told by an American general and a British brigadier to withdraw back to his previous position. Two days later, with the Germans now firmly entrenched, he was ordered to retake the hill. His troops suffered heavy casualties and he was wounded and captured, later remarking how chivalrous the Germans were – a word so appropriate to him. They patched him up and apologised for handing him over to the Italians, who had a bad reputation with prisoners of war. Fortunately, Bob was placed in a nunnery in Naples, where he recovered under the nuns' care, although he later said "At one time, I had the feeling they wanted me to die, so they could pray for my soul."

Bob was in Malaya from 1948 to 1950 during the insurgency, gaining a reputation for his outstanding leadership and navigation in the difficult jungle terrain and was Mentioned in Despatches.

In 1951, he married Mary Lynsay and they had three children.

After his last military job as attaché with the embassy in Stockholm, Sweden, he retired with the rank of Colonel.

He became a Justice of the Peace on the Newbury bench and for many years was a driver handing out "meals on wheels", often to those rather younger than himself.

When it was suggested to his daughter, Elizabeth, that Bob remained bitter about the unnecessary loss of his men, and never forgave the American military, as well as despising the brigadier and his regiment, she said: "No. No he got on well with the Americans at Greenham Common," a moment later adding: "Mind you they were Air Force, not Army."

After Mary's death in 2000, and now in his eighties, Bob decided to sell his house and divide some of the proceeds and contents between his three children, who all had families.

He moved to Hinton Court, where he could be seen daily walking in the grounds with his Labrador, Rommel. Originally, he was going to be called Monty, but Bob's admiration for the German general was greater and at times he found himself reminded of his gratitude to the Germans, who had saved his life.

One day, when they walked past the Studio and heard extraordinary sounds emitting from it, Rommel barked, not aggressively but more as if to say "we're here". Bob waved as a woman emerged and responded with a friendly smile and uplifted hand. The recently-installed new occupant of the Studio was Camilla Cochrane, and the sounds were from a recording of a humpbacked whale. Bob had been told that Camilla was one of the world's foremost inter-preters of "whale song"; their communications that travel for miles under the oceans.

The Studio was accustomed to diverse occupants and accepted various "ambiences", but nothing like the present one. No family photos on beautiful furni-ture, everything with a practical function – some would say not just untidy but chaotic, the emphasis being more technical than domestic – sound equip-ment and recording machines dotted about.

Camilla was a descendent of Thomas, Lord Cochrane (1776 – 1860), who became the 10th Earl of Dundonald. His life has been described as more extraordinary than that of Nelson; outshining his fictional counterparts, C S Forester's Horatio Horn-blower and Patrick O'Brian's Jack Aubrey. He became a household name in 1800 when he commanded a brig , the *Speedy*, and created mayhem in the Mediter-ranean, earning a fortune in prize money. With his skill as a sailor and mastery of gunnery, he was successful against ships many times the size of the *Speedy*, and was called "The Sea Wolf" by Napoleon.

His life on land was equally dramatic. Campaigning against corruption in the Admiralty, he made enemies, was framed in a Stock Exchange fraud and imprisoned; an episode exploited for Jack Aubrey by Patrick O'Brian. Cochrane escaped from prison and became a mercenary admiral. In a series of dramatic actions, famous for their disregard of formidable risks, he helped liberate Chile, Peru and Brazil from colonial rule. On reading the newspaper accounts in 1821, Lord Byron, a leading light in the movement to liberate Greece, wrote: "There is no man I envy so much as Lord Cochrane."

Returning home he became a radical MP and found enduring fame and respect amongst his countrymen.

Camilla, who was proud of her ancestor, would have made him smile. Regarded as an eccentric, from an early age she was a fanatical birdwatcher and naturalist, becoming a writer for ornithological magazines. On the outbreak of war in 1939, still a teenager, she volunteered to be a "plane spotter". This involved using powerful binoculars to identify and report incoming enemy aircraft: Heinkels, Dorniers, Junkers, Focke-Wulfs and Messerschmits, so that appropriate fighter aircraft could be scrambled to meet them. Soon after joining the Observer Corps, Camilla showed her grasp of the job and was congratulated by the instructors, to whom she said with a smile: "Birds, being smaller than aircraft, are more difficult to keep in focus." She was posted to the Isle of Wight and became a big success.

It was during her course in Portsmouth that she met Peter Taylor, a young Fleet Air Arm Pilot and they became engaged. His Fairey Swordfish aircraft, having flown from HMS *Ark Royal,* dropped its torpedo which hit the pride of the German navy, the battleship *Bismarck*, causing minor damage as her armour was half a metre thick. Mortifyingly, Peter was shot down, and his body was never recovered from the sea.

Camilla was approached many times, but possible suitors quickly realised this attractive young woman was not going to show a green light. She kept Peter's engagement ring on her finger for the rest of her life.

In her late seventies, with no family, she decided to downsize from her large house. She had visited a friend in Hinton Court and liked the idea of becoming a resident – independent but with back up facilities.

The Studio, distant from the nursing home, was perfect for Camilla. On the day of her arrival, a pair of herons flew lazily overhead. She hung all available trees with bird feeders and placed a large birdbath in her kitchen eyeline. The robins soon came to eat from her hand and, in addition to the usual varieties of tits and finches, there were nuthatches and greater spotted wood-peckers on the feeders. Overhead, buzzards would float on the thermals and kestrels inspected the Studio, where house martins nested under the eaves. On the ground she saw pheasants, partridges, green woodpeckers and wagtails, with foxes, roe deer, muntjac, scurrying hedgehogs and the inevitable rabbits and pigeons. She tolerated the grey squirrels, who visited her feeders, finding ingenious ways of defeating their anti-squirrel designs.

One June morning, while she was having breakfast, a flash of pink settled on the grass 55 feet from her window (she later measured the distance). The previous day, she had heard and been puzzled by an unusual sound from the nearby stand of large Norwegian maples, a low resonating "pooo-poo" which she decided was not a pigeon but could not be a hoopoe – a very rare visitor. But here the bird was to her delight. Described in the RSPB Handbook of British Birds: *26-28cm, smaller than a town pigeon. This exotic-looking species is slim with a long neck, long down-curved bill and crest that may be raised or lowered. Body pinkish buff with bold black and white bars on wings, tail and back. Long pinkish crest is tipped with black and is laid flat most of the time.*

Camilla became a popular character, generous in helping other residents – taking them in her old battered Volkswagen Beetle into Salisbury to shop.

Her illustrated lecture *Whale Song* will long be remembered by those who attended it. She explained, with recordings, how the 14 metre humpback whales made their emotional communications, with a mixture of mournful sighs and squeals, that were structured, intricate and precise. Camilla contrasted the bellowing males, who sing most during their six-month mating season, with the whisperings of a mother to her calf. She demonstrated how the whales listened to one another and improvised like jazz musicians, and with her final recording showed the manner with which they mirrored the Sonata form by establishing a theme, a variation, and then a return to the original theme.

At her funeral, friends were surprised to find three strange elderly men in their midst; in plain clothes but, by their bearing, possibly from the military. An inspection of the order of service revealed that a retired Air Commodore was to give a tribute.

From the pulpit his words explained that Camilla's work had been a factor in winning the war. Not as significant as the cracking of the "Enigma" code, but none the less an important contribution to the success of the Battle of Britain. "Our early superiority in the use of radar to help the fight against the Luftwaffe is well known. Less well known is that it worked in conjunction with the plane spotters of the Observer Corps, of whom Camilla was an important operator. She astounded the Air Ministry with the accuracy, detail and swiftness of her reports of approaching enemy aircraft.

"Air Marshall Dowding, in a dispatch after the Battle of Britain, said that: 'The work of the Observer Corps was invaluable. Without it, the air raid warning systems could not have been operated and inland interceptions would rarely have been made.' As a result of their role, in 1941 they became the Royal Observer Corps.

"In 1943, Camilla Cochrane was awarded an OBE (Military) for her outstanding service. From your reaction, I see that not many of you knew of this honour. She was a remarkable woman."

A particular friend of Camilla Cochrane's was Jimmy Quinn, who served in the same squadron of Fairey Swordfish as Peter Taylor. Jimmy, with his young wife Daphne, became very close friends and after Peter's death they had been the main comforters of Camilla. Over the years they never lost touch and on Daphne's death from cancer, it was Camilla's turn to comfort Jimmy and a platonic but loving relationship ensued. After he had visited Hinton Court a number of times he rang to say he had decided to move there. She was delighted.

Jimmy had had a good war, receiving a Distinguished Service Cross (DSC) and an Air Flying Cross (AFC) as well as a Croix de Guerre from the French. With Peter in the same attack on the *Bismarck*, it was a torpedo from Jimmy's Fairey Swordfish that hit the battleship's stern, damaging her steering to an extent that allowed the Home Fleet to catch and sink her.

After the war, as a young Lieutenant Commander he was made Acting Commander and second in command of an Air Station. He soon realised that the Captain was seriously incompetent and reported him to the Admiralty. He was told that if he insisted in pursuing his claim it could be detrimental to his career. Jimmy felt it his duty to the Service and the personnel at the Air Station to make sure the Captain was replaced. Like the whistleblowers of today, who instead of being rewarded, or even thanked, are often sidelined and find themselves blackballed, Jimmy's official record was marked and aged 40 , he was a "passed over" Lieutenant Commander soon due for retirement. (After eight years as a Lieutenant, promotion to Lieutenant Commander is automatic, after that, by Admiralty selection.)

His last appointment was to HMS Falcon, the Royal Naval Air Station (RNAS) at Hal Far in Malta GC - now no more.

When the government decided the defence budget had to be severely cut, there was a bit of a war between the services as to who should make the greatest sacrifices. The Admiralty sent out a request for volunteers to take early retirement. This became known as "Sandys' Axe", Duncan Sandys being the Minister of Defence. Those who were voluntarily axed received a lump sum in addition to their pensions. Among them was Jimmy Quinn.

Years later, a now retired Commander, who served with Jimmy in Malta, wrote to a friend:

In the wardroom for the officers' children's party, Jimmy's Father Christmas, after he had had a drink or two, was hilarious, but some of the children found him rather frightening.

"When he got his pension plus a good lump sum with his 'Golden Bowler', the consensus of opinion in the wardroom was that once in civvy street dear old Jimmy would drink himself to death. What actually happened was that he became a teetotaller, used the money to learn about insurance and set up his own brokerage business in Esher.

After five years the floor below his offices was vacated, so he took it and set up a 'Hollerith Punch Card' business with a bevy of girls. When I left the Navy he kindly offered me the job, with a good salary, of managing the girls. This I accepted with gratitude. By then he was sharing an aeroplane with Jack Brabham, the Formula One racing driver, and changing his Bentley every other year.

In particular, I will always remember the day, when I was a Lieutenant, before the request for voluntary retirements, when Jimmy asked me if I'd like to fly with him. I said yes, thank you, but please no aerobatics. Having had lengthy instructions about what to do in an emergency, I climbed into the back seat of a Meteor jet. With the canopy shut my 'Bone Dome' pushed against it so I had to lean forward rather uncomfortably. There could be no doubt that Jimmy was a very good pilot. I was soon being treated to a 'Farnborough' exhibition of aerobatics with the added frisson of a sea level approach to Dingli Cliffs and at the last moment a swoop up over the top. Yes I was frightened but I will never forget the flight and managed not to be sick. What could I say after landing, climbing out, shaken and angry and then seeing Jimmy's grin. I was told after-

wards that in addition to being mad to fly with Jimmy,
with his drink problem, the Meteor was an unpopular
aircraft as a number of them had blown up in mid air
for, at the time, no explained reason.
These reminiscences of Jimmy Quinn bring affec-
tionate smiles. Will cast off now. Yours, Edward."

At Hinton Court, Jimmy Quinn did not join the book club, art group, or enlist with the bridge players. But he enjoyed the croquet and became a much appreciated and remembered "Entertainer" at parties and celebrations, with his music hall songs, George Formby impression, and particularly, his finale; a tear-jerking rendition of 'Clementine'. All accompanied by his four-stringed ukulele; the name of which is taken from the Hawaiian for "Leaping Flea".

CHAPTER 14

Hester had expressed surprise when Barbara Beaty, the famous author, known as much for her partying and lively life as her books, had asked if she could visit. Hester had recently read an article about her which pointed out that in spite of being expelled from school aged 14, and without any qualifications, she had been awarded many literary prizes and had been on the Booker shortlist three times. The last time there were many who told her she would win, so she admitted there was a momentary low when she did not.

Compared to many popular authors, she was known as being very modest, confessing her ignorance and being unsure of her merits.

Now, here she was, sitting opposite Hester, somewhat ravaged looking and asking if she minded her smoking. Hester said "that's fine," and after a moment watching her light up, commented: "I've read and admired nearly all your books, but don't understand why you want to join us here?"

Barbara, having drawn on her cigarette, replied.

"From my past work maybe you would expect me to visit a National Health establishment and not your Hinton Court, which has such good reports. Indeed, for my last effort, I needed to check in to a Salvation Army hostel, in a tough area, for research. There I was advised to put the bed legs on top of my shoes to keep them safe.

"I thought it would be interesting, now I'm in my seventies, to sample a more comfortable life, and possibly write about the residents. I'm sure you've got some characters from privileged backgrounds with interesting histories behind them. If I do write something, I'll let you check it before it's published. The place and people will have fictitious names."

Hester nodded. "So, from what you've just said, am I right in thinking that you are not proposing to settle here; basically you want to do research for your next book?"

Barbara nodded an affirmative.

"People anticipate spending their last years here – dying in their residence, the nursing home, hospice or hospital. If other residents suspected you were here for a short haul and would depict them in one of your books, they might not be enthusiastic to have you join them."

Barbara, having stubbed out her cigarette, stood up with a smile. "You said you admired my books, well I very much admire the way you've handled this

meeting, and who knows, I may end up here perma-
nently one day." She then held out her hand to shake
Hester's.

A few days later Barbara Beaty's latest book
arrived. Inscribed inside: *For Hester. Thank you for an
instructive and worthwhile meeting. Good luck with all your
endeavours. Barbara.*

CHAPTER 15

The years rolled by and Hinton Court's high reputation continued. Hester Harvey's two children gave her joy. Son, Roger, got into the Royal Naval College, Dartmouth, and was set for a successful career. Daughter, Harriet, became a nurse and then spent the necessary years qualifying as a doctor, showing an interest in eventually taking over Hinton Court.

There had inevitably been the occasional hiccup, but thankfully none with a destructive consequence.

Hermione Blackmore was constantly complaining that the cleaners were not up to standard. (Now known as 'domestics', she would sarcastically say, just like the 'stokers' on her late husband's aircraft carrier, who became known as 'mechanical engineers').

It took a member from that marvellous community in Nepal, the Gurkhas, with more VCs than any other regiment, to cope with Hermione Blackmore. A Gurkha Brigade, with their married quarters, was stationed near Hinton Court, and one day Kamala, a Gurkha wife, arrived and met the head warden. In good English, she said she had seen an advertisement in Salisbury requiring 'domestic staff'. She and a colleague would like to offer their services. After an introductory course, to the delight of Hester, the staff and residents (bar one), they proved to be excellent.

When Kamala was once told "You haven't done a good job." she calmly asked "For example?" The answer came: "The oven." Kamala walked over to the oven and opened the door: it was spotless. Hermione Blackmore was astonished, and about to explode, when inexplicably she laughed, apologised and said "thank you". A phone call followed to the head warden, requesting, not demanding, that she always have Kamala. An extraordinary relationship followed. It seemingly appeared as if the Gurkha was now the boss.

In the agreement signed by the residents, para 4.4 states that *The Resident shall not cause nuisance or annoyance to other residents or staff*, and 4.5: *The Resident will take proper care to protect and avoid damage to the accommodation and communal facilities and all furnishings and decorations therein.* Para 8.1 states: *The proprietor may terminate this agreement by notice in writing where the accommodation charge or any other additional services invoiced remain unpaid for a period in excess of thirty days from the date payment was due.*

Mrs Margaret Lambert, in the stable block's 1971

Derby Winner's 'Mill Reef', had been given warning under clause 4.4 of her agreement. She had ranted and raged at lunchtime and refused to pay the accommodation charge. Hester approached her next of kin, listed as her daughter, to ask her to voluntarily remove her mother, rather than go through a legal procedure, harmful to both.

This was emphasised that same evening when Margaret Lambert was reported by a neighbouring resident to be heard trashing her accommodation, and then seen leaving 'Mill Reef' stark naked. Staff quickly found her and dealt with the situation.

A doctor's report diagnosed dementia and recommended immediate removal to a suitable nursing home. This the daughter managed to achieve.

A happier outcome for a popular male resident was made possible by Hester. Peter Portman, an atheist who died aged 97, had stipulated that on his death he was to be placed in the cheapest body bag, taken straight to the crematorium and disposed of with no family present, or service. His ashes to be collected in the cheapest container and placed under a sapling oak tree.

Peter had shown an appendix to his will to Hester, who had agreed to carry it out. When approached by his son Patrick, he was surprised she had anticipated his request, on behalf of his late father. This was to provide a marquee in the grounds adjacent to 'The

Studio', his late residence, on a Sunday as soon as convenient after his death, to accommodate sixty, including other residents, with a meal provided by James, Hinton Court's excellent chef, and plenty of wine.

For a very reasonable price, Hester was happy to provide everything: staff, furniture, cutlery and glasses, food and drink, microphone and dance floor. Patrick would book a four piece band. There were to be Quaker style speeches, complimentary or derogatory, by anyone who felt like speaking. The weather was fine and all agreed that it was a suitable and successful farewell for Peter who would have been pleased.

Hester always signed her memos "HRH", to the amusement of her admiring and respectful staff, who treated her like royalty.

After a protracted series of treatments, she died from cancer, having first handed the reins of Hinton Court to her daughter, Harriet, to be assisted by Harriet's husband, also a doctor, and Dr Sam Harvey, her father.

After a conventional funeral in a packed Hinton church, came a well attended memorial service in Salisbury cathedral, offered by the Dean who felt that it was no more than Hester's due, as she had been the benefactor of so many local charities, helping others to achieve their dreams.

A particular example was her gift of land on the

Northwest side of Hinton Court's twenty acres, to a company who were looking for a site to build a hospice for terminally ill children.

A decision was made to name it after the donor's daughter "Harriet House", and an annual donation of 12 red roses would be given to Hester Harvey. On her death the custom continued, with the roses being placed on her grave.

SOURCES

A Childhood in Scotland by Christian Miller
Amesbury Abbey Group (Care Homes)
Army Flying Museum, Middle Wallop
Art Quarterly
Beautiful and Beloved by Roderick Owen with Tristan de
Vere Cole
Campaign for Dignity in Dying
Cochrane by Robert Harvey
The Duchess of Jermyn Street by Daphne Fielding
Equity Magazine
Funeral and Memorial Elegies
The Last Bastard? by Tristan de Vere Cole
The Oldie
Reynolds Stone by Humphrey Stone
Thinking Faces Janet Stone in Conversation with
Jonathan Gili
The Times
Daily Telegraph
Guardian
Independent
Thomas Girtin by David Hill
Those Magnificent Women by Giles Whittell
Wikipedia
Women in The War by Lucy Fisher

ACKNOWLEDGMENTS

For their input, my thanks to:

Jim Radley
Liisa Steele
Katherine Calvocoressi
And Anne Stow

ABOUT THE AUTHOR

Tristan de Vere Cole, born in 1935, is generally acknowledged to be the last illegitimate child of Augustus John (1878-1961). He grew up with the artist's family and travelled to the West Indies and Europe with them in the pre-war years.

After two years training at the Royal Naval College, Dartmouth, he served a further seven years, leaving in 1960.

He first toured as an assistant stage manager with Cleo Laine's jazz revue *Here is the News*. He then worked at the Bristol Old Vic as actor and assistant stage manager, before beginning his career in television. Becoming a BBC drama director in 1966, he worked on programmes as varied as *Z Cars, Doctor Who, Secret Army, Bergerac, Howard's Way,* the four-part classic serial *Kenilworth* and the five-part *John Halifax Gentleman*.

"Scott's *Kenilworth*, beautifully made over... was exceptionally lively and lustrous."
Maurice Wiggin, *The Sunday Times*

"*John Halifax Gentleman* is just perfect. Thank you... I have known and loved the book for years, and so often when one knows a book as well as that, any adaptation can be a disappointment. In this case, however, I wouldn't have changed a word or an actor... I would so like to thank you for your sensitive direction."

A viewer's letter.

ALSO BY TRISTAN de VERE COLE

Beautiful and Beloved

(The life of Mavis de Vere Cole)

With Roderic Owen

Hutchinson, 1974

A Guide for Actors New to Television

Element Books, 1985

The Last Bastard?

2015

"My understanding of the life and work of Augustus John and characters such as Sir Mortimer Wheeler has been substantially enhanced. An absolute gem."

Dr Maredudd ap Huw, National Library of Wales.

"I devoured **The Last Bastard?** *in one long enjoyable gulp… It is all gripping stuff and very well written."*

Nicholas Shakespeare.

The Television Years

2017

In preparation:

Four Centuries of British Women Artists

Dorelia

(The life of Dorelia McNeill, Augustus John's muse and partner for over 50 years)

Printed in Great Britain
by Amazon